P9-BZB-923

Stephen King's "The Body":

BOOKMARKED

AARON BURCH

Kirby Gann, *Series Editor*

PUBLISHING

NEW YORK, NY

Copyright © 2016 by Aaron Burch.
All rights reserved.

No part of this book may be used or reproduced in any manner without written permission of the publisher. Please direct inquiries to:

Ig Publishing
Box 2547
New York, NY 10163
www.igpub.com

ISBN: 978-1-63246-030-1

PRINTED IN THE UNITED STATES OF AMERICA

FIRST EDITION | FIRST PRINTING

My brain's the cliff, and my heart's the bitter buffalo.
—"Heart Cooks Brain," Modest Mouse

People tend to claim "the book was better than the movie," but writers will accept influence from any medium, anywhere, at any time, so long as it provides fuel for the imagination. Life works the way it does and typically we don't get to choose what affects us most dramatically, what sticks deep in our consciousness and grabs hold and won't let go.

Especially when it comes to the category that falls under the header of the *First Time*—the first kiss, the first time passing an entire night alone in an empty house, the first touch of alcohol or some other soon-to-be beloved drug, the first day at school—that inventory of experiences in which we know instantly that what we believed to be true about life in general and ourselves in particular is heretofore transformed irrevocably. A guitarist's first listen to Jimi Hendrix or Doc Watson. A painter's first time before an actual Van Gogh. A novelist's first reading of a work that challenges and changes all assumptions of what the novel can do, or be.

Maybe one of the most profound firsts for most of us is that which lies at the heart of Stephen King's celebrated novella: the first encounter with a corpse—that dull fact of useless matter left behind once a human being passes on. The strangeness emanating from a human body that had once been alive, capable of friendship and worry and wonder just as we are; the bizarre metamorphosis of a living person now transformed into the inanimate, an object. It's kind of weird.

Of course "The Body," and its subsequent (and surprisingly faithful) rendering into film by the director Rob Reiner, *Stand by Me*, are less about the encounter with a dead stranger than they are about the journey four young boys make to see the body beside some railroad tracks. Both works explore the nature of nostalgia and the peculiar purity of childhood friendship, and, without over-sentimentalizing the subject, how an action that began simply as something to do on a summer day can end up becoming the defining event in one's life.

One refreshing aspect of Aaron Burch's exploration here is its honesty: how many would readily cop to the fact that the movie version of a fictional work started his own journey as a writer, that a *film* fed his fundamental notions of storytelling, his lifelong thematic preoccupations? King's novella came to Burch only later, and, colored already by what had been seen, the text's primary value—for a time, at least—lay in how well it informed and compared with the movie that spoke to a young Aaron so deeply; the prose version of the story appears to have required more time for its unique impact and influence to make themselves known to the author-in-progress. This tension between the film-version and the word-version feeds a grand autobiographical accounting of the many ways in which a fundamental story can resonate in various manifestations, affecting one not only in terms of a developing creative vision but also in the creation of one's life.

Kirby Gann
June 2016

1

I was twelve going on thirteen when I first saw *Stand By Me.* I guess that would have made it 1990. As the narrator, Gordie Lachance, in a voiceover at the beginning of the film, says about the first time he saw a dead human being: "a long time ago . . . but only if you measure in terms in years." This was slightly tweaked from the first chapter of "The Body," the Stephen King novella the movie is based on: "*a long time ago . . . although sometimes it doesn't seem that long to me.*"

I have seen the movie many times over the last twenty-five years; more than the novella, it is what I've most often referenced, both in my writing and in my life. It was formative, though whether that is because of the movie itself: the actors, the soundtrack, the cinematography; or the story; or just because of the moment in my own life when I saw it, I'm not sure. I will admit that that uncertainty might be part of the magic. At least a small part of me fears what might happen when applying analysis to something held so close to the heart, by asking either too many questions, or maybe just the *right* questions. As King himself writes in that same first chapter of "The Body":

The most important things lie too close to wherever your secret heart is buried, like landmarks to a treasure your enemies would love to steal away. And you may make revelations that cost you dearly only to have people look at you in a funny way, not understanding what you've said at all, or why you thought it was so important that you almost cried while you were saying it. That's the worst, I think.[1]

---

1. This entire first chapter, unlike any other in the novella, is italicized.

2

We had a small house with a big yard, kind of on the outskirts of Lakewood, Washington. Unincorporated through my elementary and middle school years, Lakewood was then still a part of Tacoma, though pretty large to technically be a piece of something else. It's a city now, with everything "incorporation" brings with it—government, its own police and fire departments. Progress. Growing up, it felt like both part of somewhere else and not, neither city nor suburb. There were a lot of lakes, with rich people living on and around them, and then lots of sketchy areas, with pawn shops and adult bookstores; occasionally you'd see an episode of *Cops* that had been filmed there. And in between, these pockets of neighborhoods where my friends and I grew up, pockets that seemed like the perfect place to be growing up. Whether I actually realized that then, or am only applying it now in retrospect, through the lens of distance and nostalgia, is hard to say. Maybe it didn't feel like that at the time; maybe kids growing up there now still think it feels that way.

One of my memories of this growing up is the glut of movies we watched as a family. My dad was the head gardener for the Seattle Public Library system, and I remember him always bringing home copies of VHS tapes; and when he wasn't bringing home whatever wasn't checked out, he was stopping at the local video store, or we were all going together as a family to pick out a movie. Walking up and down aisles of New Releases, Action, Comedy, is another nostalgia-tinted remembrance of something I miss.

One of the few specific memories I have from all this family movie watching is of my dad sitting me down and telling me that he and my mom wanted me to watch *Stand By Me*. They had watched it the night before, had loved it, and now wanted us all to watch it together. I don't know if that had been the plan all along—to "screen" the film to make sure it was suitable for my age—or if the idea to let me watch it had only occurred after their own viewing. I grew up relatively conservative Christian, and though "strict" would probably be too strong of a word to describe it, my brother and I didn't have free reign over what we were able to watch or listen to. Or maybe we did have free reign, but certain landscapes of that reign were discouraged. I have friends who were raised only slightly more conservative and were not allowed to watch PG-13 movies until they were literally thirteen, R not until they were seventeen. While that wasn't my experience, I still wasn't allowed to watch, say, *Friday the 13ᵗʰ* or *Nightmare on Elm Street*[2] or other movies deemed too scary or adult or otherwise inappropriate for one reason or another.[3]

---

2. First confession: I still haven't seen any of these.
3. Nor were my brother and I allowed (or, semantics notwithstanding, we were also *discouraged*) to listen to music with swearing or that was deemed "unsuitable" for other reasons that now escape me. Another of my small moments of vivid memory is an anecdote of trying to tell my

I remember my dad telling me that *Stand by Me* was a little "mature,"[4] but that he thought it was worth watching, that it was about a group of kids who were my own age, give or take, and the themes were not only good and relevant, but *important*. I remember him saying that even though they all make fun of Vern throughout the movie, they don't when it really matters. *At one point*, I remember him saying[5], *they cross a train track bridge and Vern is so scared he gets down on all fours and crawls his way across, but the other three kids, Vern's friends, understand, they get it.* You make fun of those closest to you for the little shit, not the stuff that matters.

And with that, we watched the movie.

And then . . . I don't remember the movie itself. Not that first viewing of it anyway. I remember the movie, of course; I've seen it countless times over the years, but I don't remember anything about it specific to that initial viewing. I remember my dad's introduction, his bequeathing on the movie not only his seal of approval, but his recommendation, his insinuation that there was something to be learned from it, his highlighting that it was about friendship, and that friendships are one of the most important things in life. Maybe the *most* important?

---

dad that I had borrowed "a CD" from a friend, which he kept hearing as "AC/DC"—I am unsure if I'm more surprised by the fact that maybe AC/DC was "bad" or find more humor in the SNL-skit-like number of times we had to volley that misunderstanding back and forth.

4. I don't remember him using that word specifically, but it feels most apt for the memory as it exists.

5. Either my memory here is slightly wrong, or, time-machine note to dad: um, spoiler alert.

3

For the last few years, I've taught a pair of Introductory English classes: "Writing and Literature" and "Writing and Academic Inquiry." Perhaps my biggest goal for these classes is to push each of my students to be purposeful. To think through their own writing, to analyze and make decisions about their own writer-choices. To ask questions: about the class readings, about their own writing, about themselves, about *life*. This may be a Writing class, but it is also about Academic Inquiry. "At the heart of the writing process, then, is a willingness to ask good questions," states the Preface of the textbook[6] I use. "This shift in the way students view writing—*arriving* at a position rather than beginning with one—is perhaps the most significant and exciting change they undergo at college." Maybe this is something super obvious to all Intro English teachers (before this job, I had only taught Creative Writing and Business and Technical Writing), maybe it's obvious to everyone, but it blew my mind a little when I was first exposed to it. It gave me a language to use in my classroom, an easy

---

6. *Creative Composition*, Pollack, Chamberlin, Bakopoulos.

phrase to apply to essays that didn't connect with me. Not a thesis, but a *driving question*. It explained why I myself had always struggled with theses as a student; it explained why the very few essays I'd tried to write over the years hadn't worked. "Re-proving what you already know to be true"[7] is boring. "But a question implies movement."[8]

The first week of class, I always show the "Why?" clip from Louis C.K.'s HBO show, *Lucky Louie*.

"Can I play outside?" asks Louie's young daughter as they both sit at the table having their morning cereal.

"No."

"Why?"

"Because it's 5 o'clock in the morning, it's too early."

"Why?"

"The sun hasn't come up yet."

"Why?"

"Because the sun comes up later."

"Why?" she asks, again and again, and again, until finally, two and half minutes later, Louie answers, "Cause God is dead and we're alone."

"OK." His daughter finally relents.

Louis C.K.—or, I guess, technically, his daughter—I tell my students, is going to be our Patron Saint of Intro English. We are going to push our essays to become less about proving a point and more about analysis: asking questions, searching for understanding, figuring something out. We are going to get in the habit of asking "Why?" again and again, until we

---

7. Ibid.
8. Ibid.

can't ask anymore and/or we reach the end result of "God is dead and we're alone."[9]

Each of the last few years, the theme I've chosen for these classes has been "The Rhetoric of Growing Up." As I say on my syllabus, "'Rhetoric of Growing Up' because the idea of 'growing up'/'coming of age' is a common and powerful literary model and tradition."

We usually do some kind of ice breaker as way of taking roll, and either that first day of class, or maybe the second, I ask them what they think that phrase means, "coming of age." What comes to mind, what does it mean *to them*?

"Independence," someone usually says, or something along those lines. They usually start broad. "Finding yourself," "making decisions for yourself," "becoming who you are."

"Can you be more specific?"

"High school graduation." "Moving away from home." Sometimes they get super specific: "going to the bank by myself," "buying my own groceries." These are the moments they are in the middle of, having just moved away from home for the first time, beginning their first semester at college. But then, some students go younger or older, too—they talk around the ideas of puberty or having sex for the first time, though without explicitly saying either. Others say "getting married," or "having kids," like "growing up" is still something out ahead of them, in their future, not something they think

---

9. When class is going well, they laugh at this tag. When they don't . . . it's going to be a long semester.

about being in the middle of, answering this question during their very first week away from home, their first week of college; sometimes, schedule depending, even their very first college class.

This, too, I tell them, is one of the reasons why I like it as theme for the class. Because of its malleability as a phrase, "growing up" can be applied to almost whatever you want; it can be used as catchall. It can be (back to my own syllabus), "a means of exploring various issues and constructs (race, ethnicity, gender, sexuality, religious affiliation, regional background, economic status)," which also means I can throw in almost any reading I want, and still claim it is "on theme."

And, finally, I chose "coming of age" because they are probably my favorite kinds of stories. "One of the benefits of being a teacher," I tell my students, "is getting to make you talk about what I like."[10]

But, then: Why do I love so coming of age stories?

Why *Stand By Me*, why "The Body"?

---

10. Again: good classes hopefully at least chuckle here.

4

Directed by Rob Reiner, *Stand By Me* was released in 1986, four years after publication of Stephen King's *Different Seasons*, the collection of four novellas that included "The Body." At this point in his career, King had been publishing novels for almost a decade, since the publication of *Carrie* in 1974, and he would go on to publish at least a book a year between then and now, going on forty years and counting.

King notes in *Different Seasons'* Afterword that, "each of these longish stories was written immediately after completing a novel—it's as if I've always finished the big job with just enough gas left in the tank to blow off one good-sized novella." There is "The Breathing Method," written immediately after his sixth novel, *Firestarter*; "Rita Hayworth and the Shawshank Redemption," after the novel before that, *The Dead Zone*; "Apt Pupil"[11] after *The Shining*; and the oldest

---

11. It should be noted that in a book of four novellas, three have not only been made into movies, but very good movies. *Stand By Me*, of course; *Apt Pupil* is a less exceptional, although solid, movie about an aging Nazi war criminal and his thirteen-year-old neighbor who discovers his true identity; and *Shawshank Redemption*, a movie likely many (myself included) would argue easily worthy the attention I herewith am paying almost entirely to *Stand By Me*.

novella in the collection, "The Body," written after his second novel, *'Salem's Lot*.[12]

Stand By Me starred Wil Wheaton, River Phoenix, Corey Feldman, and Jerry O'Connell as the four young boys at the heart of the story: Gordie Lachance, Chris Chambers, Teddy Duchamp, and Vern Tessio, respectively. The actors weren't much older than the roles they were playing—which wasn't much older than I was at the time of my first viewing. River Phoenix, the oldest of the four, was fifteen, two weeks shy of sixteen, when the movie was released on August 8, 1986, and O'Connell, the youngest, was only twelve and a half.

The novella, of course, came first, so it should probably be argued that one of the strengths of *Stand By Me* is how closely it adheres to its source material, how much it feels like "The Body" on the screen. I, like many, saw the movie before ever having read the story, and one of the things I love about "The Body" is how much it feels like *Stand By Me* on the page. This is to say: there are very minimal differences. As such, I find myself at times using the titles interchangeably. Except for when I'm talking around external factors—the actual life of Stephen King, as opposed to Gordon Lachance; or the actors that played the kids as opposed to the characters themselves— what I like about one is more or less mirrored in the other.

---

12. After his first book, *Carrie*, King wrote and published one other novel under his own name in this span between *Firestarter* and *'Salem's Lot*: *The Stand*. Perhaps it was *such* a "big job" he had no gas left in the tank at all. Or he found himself more quickly refilled and moved right into *The Dead Zone*. Or he was so close to empty, he sputtered out only the shorter stories of *Night Shift*. I'm not entirely sure of the gas-to-writing metaphor here. Also, for cleanliness-of-counting sake, this count does not include the novels he published during these years under the name Richard Bachman: *Rage* and *The Long Walk*.

What I love about "The Body" is often what I love about *Stand By Me*, and vice versa.

When I started this book, I made a list of topics to cover. I wrote down "nostalgia" and "deer scene," "first time I saw movie" and "first time I saw a buffalo." I wrote down *"Carrie/ Salem's Lot/ The Shining."* I haven't read any of those novels and I thought maybe I could, or even *should*. If King had "just enough gas in the tank to blow off one good-sized novella," it seemed worth looking into where the bulk of that tank of gas had been spent traveling through. Trace the path back, as it were, look for similarities, connections, find something to say about that first stage of Stephen King's career, especially as he is one of the few writers everyone is at least passingly familiar with. And, too, the Gordon Lachance of "The Body" is himself not only a writer, but a very Stephen King-like writer. What are the similarities between the career that Lachance hints at and the actual career of Stephen King (especially at the time of writing "The Body")?

But then, ultimately . . . I realized I don't care. 'Salem's Lot doesn't have anything to do with my affection for "The Body." Neither does King, really; not his career, not his reputation. I saw *Stand By Me* before I ever read "The Body," and it was the movie I initially fell in love with. As such, this book (perhaps frustratingly?) is short on literary history, on Stephen King argument. Ultimately, I love both movie and novella because of the way they handle and present friendship and coming of age, being a writer and telling a story, nostalgia and growing up. These are the topics and themes I often find myself most interested in and curious about, topics and themes that "The Body" and *Stand By Me* traffic in and handle especially well.

5

I am fascinated by beginnings. I think this has always been the case, but it has certainly amplified since I began teaching. In part because they're important, obviously; in part because they're easy to teach. Middles, endings: those take context. It's harder, if not impossible, to look at a large selection of endings, side-by-side, and analyze what works, and why. They work because of everything that came before. Conversely, beginnings work because of everything that comes after, but you don't know that yet at their time of presentation. A good beginning should pique your interest, it should make you want to read more. It should make you start asking some questions—once your brain starts inventing questions, you're involved, you have an interest, and now you want to keep reading, because questions need answers. A good beginning gives you all that and, too, in the parlance of creative writing classroom, it *teaches you how to read the piece itself.*[13]

•

_____

13. A footnote in an essay I sometimes teach, Matt Bell's "Ken Sent Me," about the video game *Leisure Suit Larry*, notes: "Like the gameplay it describes, this essay can be more than one thing, depending on the situation. This is essay as guide, as walkthrough, as reflection on personal

"The Body" (and, likewise, *Stand By Me*) starts with an adult, "present day" Gordon Lachance reflecting back on his life. "*I was twelve going on thirteen when I first saw a dead human being,*" he tells us. "*It happened in 1960[14], a long time ago . . .*" The second chapter then flashes back, to Gordie and his two friends, Teddy and Chris, playing three-penny-scat ("the dullest card-game ever invented, but it was too hot to think about anything more complicated") and telling jokes ("How do you know when a Frenchman's been in your back yard? Well, your garbage cans are empty and your dog is pregnant.") in their treehouse.

That's almost the entirety of the first two chapters, much of it simple scene-setting and description, and yet those details are littered with information that comes back throughout the rest of the novella. The roof of their treehouse is a corrugated tin sheet "hawked from the dump, looking over our shoulders all the time we were hustling it out of there, because the dump custodian's dog was supposed to be a real kid-eating monster." Gordie kills time between hands reading detective/murder stories, and he also tells us that Teddy was "the dumbest guy we hung around with, I guess, and he was crazy," that

---

experience." That blurring not only of genre but of intention, of purpose, is itself the subgenre of nonfiction I have found myself most drawn to in recent memory, and that sentence makes clear my own goal for this book. It is appreciation and analysis of "The Body" and *Stand By Me*, but also memoir—my connections to, and thoughts on, this source material, as well as my own growing up, my coming of age stories as man, writer, teacher, husband. This is book as guide, as walkthrough, as reflection on personal experience.

14. 1959, for some reason, in the movie. Also, "the first time I saw," instead of "when I first saw."

his "big thing was what he called 'truck-dodging." We also learn that Teddy's dad stormed the beach at Normandy; held the sides of Teddy's head down to cast-iron burner plates, burning both ears; and was now at Togus, a VA hospital, "where you have to go if you're section eight."

We also know that, a few months before, Gordie's brother died in a Jeep accident, and his parents hadn't recovered. "I'd been like the Invisible Boy that whole summer," Gordie says. We know that that whole summer had been "the driest and hottest since 1907," possibly the least relevant among these pieces of information and foreshadowing, but a distinction that places "The Body" alongside other great pieces of art set during the hottest summer on record or the hottest day of the year such as *The Great Gatsby* and *Do the Right Thing*.

At the end of the second chapter, another friend, Vern Tessio, enters, and now we've met all four main characters. We know one of these kids, Gordon Lachance, is telling us this story from later in his life, looking back, and we also know a lot more about Gordie and his friends and the town they live in, Castle Rock, than we even think yet relevant.

Sweaty and panting, Vern brings with him a question. Or, a couple questions. First, "Can you guys camp out tonight?" And then, "You guys want to go see a dead body?"

6

One argument: the reason "The Body"—and *Stand By Me*—work is nostalgia. The movie was released in 1986, the story set in 1960, and the songs on the movie soundtrack have a certain 1950s feel, most having been originally released in the mid-to-late fifties.

Further, it is a coming of age story, the genre most directly linked to nostalgia, and is being told by an adult narrator, looking back on his own coming of age. *Stand By Me* opens not with Wil Wheaton as Gordie Lachance, but with Richard Dreyfuss[15] as adult Gordie. "The Body" isn't written in past tense as pure point of view choice; the present of the narrator isn't implicit: we are made aware from the get-go. "*It happened in 1960, a long time ago . . .*" The second chapter opens, "We had a treehouse in a big elm which overhung a vacant lot in Castle Rock. There's a moving company on that lot today, and the elm is gone. Progress." The story itself doesn't just work

---

15. Actually, the very first time we see adult Gordie sitting in his Land Rover 109, it is David Dukes, who was originally cast as "The Writer," but later replaced by Dreyfuss.

because of a general nostalgia for the past, but is itself *about* nostalgia. Gordie is looking back on his life, telling us a story through his own lens of nostalgia. And that dominoes into us looking back on our own lives—there is the nostalgia for our own treehouses; there is the nostalgia of what used to be a vacant lot, before there was a moving company there, before there was *progress*.

Further still, for myself and many of my generation who saw the movie as kids, there is now a nostalgia for when you first saw the movie (or perhaps even first read the novella). It's nostalgia on nostalgia.

One of the most famous TV moments of the last decade is the final scene from the first season of *Mad Men*. In the episode titled, "The Carousel," Don Draper is pitching company men from Kodak how he'd advertise their new "wheel," the donut-shaped machine that holds and projects slides and can be arranged in a prearranged sequence and clicked through, as slideshow. "Nostalgia," Draper says. "It's delicate . . . but potent. Teddy told me that in Greek, 'nostalgia' literally means 'the pain from an old wound.' It's a twinge in your heart, far more powerful than memory alone."

"It happened in 1960, a long time ago . . . although sometimes it doesn't seem that long to me," Gordie Lachance tells us, the *potency* of nostalgia collapsing time. *"Especially on the nights I wake up from dreams where the hail fall into his open eyes,"* the first chapter ends, the pain from Lachance's old wound still lingering in his dreams. That's the power of nostalgia: it can make "a long time ago" seem like not that long at all; it's the idea Draper grabs hold of to sell the Kodak men of the very power of their own product.

•

I was born in Ojai, California, my brother was born four years later in Salinas, and we moved from California to Washington State a couple years after that, where we lived in a few different houses, in a few different towns, until, in 1987, when I was nine, my family moved into the house that I would live in until I moved into a dorm for college. I don't remember much from anywhere before that, any of the houses before I was nine; I lived in that house for ten years, the longest I've ever lived in one residence. It was, simply, the house I grew up in. The house in which I remember watching *Stand By Me* for the first time, on the couch in the living room, the living room that stayed more or less the same until my parents bought a new, bigger house, and moved a couple of years after I went to college. I remember watching *Cheers* and *Family Ties* as a family in that living room. I remember watching *The Wonder Years*, the low-fi, "home movie" opening credits of which are still vivid in my mind; they, perhaps even more than any photos of my own childhood and family growing up, are what I recall when watching Don Draper's family photo slideshow at the end of "The Carousel."

I remember, too, watching movies by myself in that living room, when my parents went to the store and left me home alone: *Basic Instinct*, *Total Recall* (specifically, the three-breasted woman scene, obviously). I remember my parents having the "sex talk" with me there; and also, years later, I remember crying and telling them about the car accident I was a passenger in, telling them I know it didn't make sense why both my friend and I were in the backseat, leaving the front passenger seat empty, but that was the truth, leaving out that it was empty because another friend had been in that seat, the girl's boyfriend, but we'd already dropped him off and they weren't supposed to be dating, and that part of the story didn't seem to have anything to do with the car accident so why get them in trouble for that?

It is the house that I myself look back on most nostalgically, the house we left every summer or two to drive south to visit the family we'd left in California. We would pack into our station wagon and take two days to drive the fourteen hours from Lakewood, Washington to southern California, to visit grandparents, and aunts and uncles, cousins, and also the places my parents were nostalgic for. We would go on driving tours, through and past towns they grew up in, houses they'd lived in, schools they'd gone to, fast food places they'd worked at, fast food places they'd gone to with friends, lingered at, hung out at, flirted with others at, flirted with each other at. I remember my dad looking around, telling us everything that had changed. How different everything had become. *Progress*.

At the time, while it seemed like they—my dad especially—were showing my brother and I these places, telling us these stories, for our benefit, I wasn't sure what I was supposed to take away, why I should care. Now, of course, I realize they'd been as much, if not more, for my dad, as for my brother and I. As I've gotten older, I've felt these same impulses myself. I've driven my wife and stepdaughter past the house in Lakewood, I've pointed out where I went to high school, where my friends and I would skate, where things are in places that used to be vacant, where things used to be that are now gone. Progress.

"This device isn't a spaceship," Don Draper says, clicking through the slides of his own family photos. "It's a time machine." *Click*. "It goes backwards, forwards." *Click*. "It takes us to a place where we ache to go again." *Click*. "It's not called the Wheel. It's called a Carousel." *Click*. "It lets us travel the way a child travels." *Click*. "Around and around, and back home again . . . to a place where we know we are loved."

7

"Eulogy for Barnes & Noble #2628: A Personal History," by Aaron Burch. Originally published in The Rumpus, March 27, 2012. Used by Permission.

The bookstore I worked at in college recently closed. I hadn't thought of the store in probably a few years, hadn't set foot inside in considerably longer. It wasn't even something cool and indie, with a storied history or a local celebrity of a quirky owner, but a Barnes & Noble. I read the news via the nearly emotionless ticker of Facebook, and it surprised me that it affected me at all. It was sadder than seemed reasonable, maybe; sadder than I would have expected, certainly.

My sophomore year in college, after moving out of the dorm and into a house with friends, I found myself needing money for rent, for food. My best friend, and one of many roommates (there were, like, nine of us; college!), knew a guy who worked at the Barnes & Noble down the hill from us, in University Village, and they were hiring.

Walking in to ask for an application was more than a little overwhelming. I'd only been in mall stores like Walden's, or used bookstores, or the Borders in Tacoma, but that was really only for music. Their CDs were more expensive than anywhere else, but they somehow got more imports and rare stuff than anyone else. The Borders was the closest relation, of course, but this Barnes & Noble felt cleaner, better organized, more inviting. There was more space in between the shelves of books, or at least something about the layout of the store made it seem like there was, so you could walk and browse without feeling trapped or claustrophobic when others were nearby. Big, comfortable chairs welcomed you to sit and read and treat the store like something other than just commerce, and skylights kept the store naturally bright instead of the harshness of workplace fluorescence. And it was big. Much bigger than the Borders, though we always bee-lined from the entrance to the music section, leaving the rest of the store almost negligible and overall seeming even smaller than it was. This B&N had two stories—three (two-and-a-half?), if you counted the mezzanine, with the café and a couple of dozen tables for people to read, students to do homework. I remember hearing it was one of the biggest bookstores west of the Mississippi (top five?), or maybe just one of the biggest Barnes & Nobles, or maybe that's some kind of lame, misremembered bookstore rumor. Walking in for the first time felt a little like the first day at a new school, like you were bound to get lost and would never be able to quite figure it all out. (I hadn't yet been to Powell's, only a few hours south.)

I'd recently read *Fight Club* and *The Beach* back-to-back, which, in the spirit of remembering, I credit largely for throwing me into my love of reading. I'd grown up reading Matt Christopher's sports books and The Hardy Boys and a number of the *Choose Your Own Adventure* series, but not with the fervor or dedication that in the years since has been re-appropriated from super geeky to kind of cool. In middle and high school, I don't remember reading all that much, aside from *Beckett Baseball Card Monthly* and *Nintendo Power*, becoming more interested in, well, baseball cards and Nintendo. And movies. These two recent reads, in fact, had both been discovered through *Entertainment Weekly*: one because the movie rights had been optioned by the guy that did *Seven* and *Alien 3*, the other by the guys behind *Trainspotting* and *Shallow Grave*. Which is all to say, I liked books and reading fine, but the possibility of working at a bookstore mostly just seemed better than fast food.

My friend and I both applied. I got the job.

During my first week—training or orientation or whatever it was called—everything continued to overwhelm. I had to memorize the store number, which was the code to the employee backroom, and also phone numbers, and my employee number to clock in and out, and where all the sections were. Cooking and Sports and Self-Help and History, Audio Books and Large Print and Travel, with its guidebooks and maps and foreign language guides (audio and text) to accompany and help with said travel. Keeping track of it all seemed like having to memorize a poem or lines for a play. I understood, of course, the overarching differences between Fiction and Non, and what was what, but not the language or specifics; it seems hard to believe, and embarrassing to admit, the number of times I had to remind myself: if it was not fact, it was fiction, if it was fact, it was nonfiction. (Herein lies another whole argument but, c'mon, you know what I mean.) One of those first couple of days, we were being given a tour of the store and I still vividly remember one of the fellow new hires recognizing a name on a book at the far end of the new release wall and pointing it out as someone he'd worked with at some previous job, in some different state, years before. I remember thinking that seemed cool, seeing a book on a bookshelf by someone you knew.

I learned to work a cash register, which is easy, and I'm good at and like math so was even kind of fun, but this was only my second job, and the first was at a produce warehouse, so all these tasks were new and had to be learned and seemed as foreign at first as, well, learning a foreign language, the section for which was ... in the back corner, just past religion? Or was it upstairs? And then, all of a sudden, it was second nature and I won multiple "contests" by my till being correct the most days in a row. And, like by the second or third week at a new school, the store already seemed small and familiar and how could I have ever gotten lost there? I passed my time by paying attention to what people bought. I learned to scorn the bestsellers, the books bought most often by moms and other customers I presumed to be the opposite of myself; made note and set aside copies of books bought by people who looked cool or who also bought music or movies I liked. This wasn't before the Internet, but was certainly before the Internet was used for everything (I didn't yet own my own computer, and I checked my new university email on a DOS program in campus computer labs), and I scanned daily the books-in-print and bookstore distributor programs on the cash register computers for updates on a new Palahniuk or Garland.

For the next couple of years, this job was how I paid for

rent, for food, for all the cheap beer you drink only when in college. The job also saved me money on textbooks that we normally wouldn't carry but that I ordered for myself and then bought with my employee discount. The job supplied me with books to read for pleasure; I met my college girlfriend. Her being an English major confused me, both because what was she going to do with such a degree, but also because I was still all kinds of undecided. School was something I was doing so I could finish and be done with and then figure out what I wanted to do, while she had a senior seminar class entirely focused on the work of one contemporary author I'd never heard of, which seemed kind of cool but also not like a real thing.

At work, I bought books by Michael Chabon and Tim Sandlin and Denis Johnson, after they were recommended by customers or co-workers. I frequently took home *The New Yorker*, especially when I timed it right and grabbed issues from the back, after they'd had their covers stripped for credit but before the rest of the magazine was recycled. It seemed like some new, great magazine that I'd discovered, like the cool indie band that still only a couple of your friends were talking about. (Had I really not previously heard of *The New Yorker*? Seriously?!) One day, helping unload magazines, I was confused and excited by *McSweeney's #4*. This was a magazine? In this weird box, with each individual story included as its own booklet? And graphs and humor and a copyright page filled with even more writing "hidden" in among the normally boring copyright information like I remembered from my favorite comic book, *The Maxx*. I was hooked. My girlfriend and I started going to readings by McSweeney's authors, Neal Pollack and Amy Fusselman and Paul Collins, and I dragged to readings by both Palahniuk and Garland, when they came to town. A coworker lent me his DVDs of *The Sopranos* and made me promise to watch. (Which isn't especially relevant to this narrative, but ... *The Sopranos!!*)

When we graduated, my girlfriend and I moved to Oakland, because she'd gone to summer school at UC Berkeley for a semester and loved it there, and could transfer to a B&N in the area (by this time, I'd quit the bookstore and was trying to make and save money with a masonry job). I liked the idea of moving away and living somewhere new and different and the Bay Area sounded just as, if not more, cool and fun as anywhere else, and I often need other people to make when and where decisions for me.

In Oakland, I discovered the hidden corners of the local bookstores (Pendragon Books and Diesel, A Bookstore) where they kept *McSweeney's* and the other weird little magazines (is that what they were? Magazines?) that published fiction. I started a website to keep myself busy in a town where I didn't know many people, called it *Hobart* because I'd always thought it might make a good band name, and having a website seemed probably as close as I was going to get to being in a band. I learned that these "magazines" were "literary journals" and I found other examples, in print and online, and my website kind of turned itself into one. Suddenly I was the editor of a literary journal. Then my relationship with my girlfriend started its downslide toward ending, so I buried myself in my website even more. I also found an online message board of writers and editors. When my girlfriend and I broke up, I moved back to Seattle. I started emailing, and then calling, and then flying to see the cute girl from the message board.

•

I haven't lived in Seattle in almost a decade, and probably haven't been anywhere near University Village in much longer. The transition from smaller and local to upscale, national stores had already started when I'd worked there, but has now completely taken over; I have no reason to shop at Crate & Barrel or Restoration Hardware when back in town visiting friends and family. I doubt anyone I knew from my time working at B&N was still there when the store closed. (I learned about the closing of the Barnes & Noble I worked via my college girlfriend posting about it on her Facebook page.)

I now live in Ann Arbor, coincidentally the home of Barnes & Noble's major competitor, Borders. At least, they were, until they went bankrupt. I went back to school and got my MFA in Creative Writing. The website that "kind of turned itself into" a literary journal, has now "kind of taken over my life," growing from website to print journal to small press, and is co-edited by the "cute girl from the message board"/my wife. As a press, we're too small for Barnes & Noble, the last, biggest chain of bookstores to bother carrying our books, and maybe there's an irony in that and maybe there isn't. I just returned from AWP, a conference with thousands of other presses that B&N is likewise unaware exist.

It's possible that I would have ended up here, no matter what. Maybe I didn't need to first move to Oakland to make moving to Michigan seem less daunting. Maybe I would have devoted my life to reading and writing regardless. Maybe what I most needed to convince me to go back to school was just some time away, and all those specific steps in between could have been any variety of different steps. (Or maybe I would have otherwise found an interest more lucrative, or less time-consuming, or both.)

Remembering all this feels related to nostalgia, something I'm often guilty of though try not to be, but not quite the same. Nostalgia makes me look back at working at Barnes & Noble fondly, but it's an appreciation for everything that it led to that makes it feel special. Or maybe that is nostalgia, and I'm arguing semantics. Appreciation, or nostalgia, or whatever it is . . . something makes it seem worthy of mourning the loss of a bookstore, even if I sometimes feel like I am supposed to not care about a "big box" bookstore closing. Supposed to celebrate, maybe even? But I like bookstores, big and small, corporate and not. And I'm doing this remembering during a break (read: being lazy, avoiding, etc.) from trying to revise (again) a novel, and thinking of that first week at Barnes & Noble reminds me how cool it would be for a friend to one day randomly find a book by me on a bookshelf, maybe even at a Barnes & Noble.

8

Each time I've taught "The Body," the aspect of the novella that most stands out for my students, the pieces that most confuse them, are the two included short stories. The first one comprises chapter seven, and is called "Stud City."[16] It is introduced with a title-page-like note—"*Stud City*, by Gordon Lachance. Originally published in *Greenspun Quarterly*, Issue 45, Fall, 1970. Used by permission."—that tells us it was written by the same Gordie who is narrating "The Body," but otherwise is wholly unrelated. Instead, it's about this guy, Chico, who thinks fondly about his dead brother, Johnny; has sex with Jane, previously a virgin; and gets in an argument with his father and stepmother. Following the story, the next chapter in "The Body" opens, "Pretty fucking melodramatic, right?" Well, yeah, it kinda is. (Although, maybe arguably not as much as describing it as "pretty fucking melodramatic.")

"Stud City" is introduced as "by Gordon Lachance," but it isn't about him. It isn't about Teddy or Chris or Vern; there's

---

16. The second, an excerpt of "The Revenge of Lard Ass Hogan," comes nine chapters later, which we'll get to.

no mention of a dead body. It comes out of nowhere; nothing seems to connect it to the first six chapters we've just read. It literally looks cut-and-pasted, air-dropped in.

"Why?" I ask my students. "Be Louie's daughter at breakfast. Why is it there? Why did Stephen King include it?"

They shrug, a kind of, *you're the teacher, you tell us* look in their eyes.

"Because the novella wasn't long enough and King got lazy and so just cut and pasted an old story he'd written when he was young?"

They laugh.[17]

Greenspun Quarterly, Issue 45, Fall 1970.

Thus, within the timeframe of the novella, ten years after the events of the "The Body," making the "*twelve going on thirteen*" of "*It happened in 1960*" Gordie now twenty-two. Which at least helps explain the melodrama, the sophomoric derivation.

It is also the first time we find out Gordie is a writer. Later, he will talk about writing as an interest even as a twelve-year-old, and later still, we will find out that present-day Gordie of

17. Although, in fact, "Stud City" was indeed a story King had written and published himself, when younger. It was published in the Fall 1969 issue of King's undergraduate literary journal, University of Maine's *Ubris* (rather than the Fall 1970 issue of *Greenspun Quarterly*), under "Steve King." For the purpose of my class, I usually don't even tell my students this, keeping the focus on what it tells us about Gordie, rather than further confusing Lachance as King. The move of using an old story within a newer, unrelated, novella is more interesting, and worthy of more, than mere footnote mention, but also feels a rabbit hole leading away from above intended purpose.

more-or-less 1975 is a Stephen King-like writer. "Stud City," in the parlance of writing, *show-don't-tell*s us of his growth as a writer. "Even now, when I read it," Gordie reflects about "Stud City," he sees

> a Gordon Lachance younger than the one living and writing now, one certainly more idealistic than the best-selling novelist who is more apt to have his paperback contracts reviewed than his books,[18] but not so young as the one who went with his friends that day to see the body of a dead kid named Ray Brower.

King's "The Body," then, is not just the story of the first time Gordie Lachance saw a dead human body with three of his best friends, but is also the larger story of Gordie's life, how he became who he did, who he is as a whole—an adult, a writer, a man.

And if this story of the first time Gordie saw a dead human being is almost an origin story of Gordon Lachance, writer, then "Stud City" might be the story of the first time he harnessed his powers. He hadn't yet figured out how to best wield them, but he'd exerted them with purpose, at least. He was practicing. "Stud City" is Gordie retelling us the story of the first time he shot spider webs from his palms, the first time he controlled the weather, the first time he caused something to burst

---

18. In fact, Stephen King would sell *Christine*—published in 1983, the year after *Different Seasons*—for one dollar, saying, "I'll take the royalties, if the book makes royalties, but I don't want to hear any more about Stephen King's monster advances."

into flames, and "pretty fucking melodramatic" is Gordie laughing at himself, at his own retelling, at how awry it had gone.

Chapter eight continues tearing down "Stud City"—it isn't just melodramatic, it is "derivative," it is "sophomoric," it is "style by Hemingway . . . theme by Faulkner." It is pretentious, he admits, but also worse: "Its attitude toward women goes beyond hostility and to a point which actually verges on actual ugliness."

"And yet," Gordie continues, "it was the first story I ever wrote that felt like *my* story—the first one that really felt *whole*, after five years of trying."

It is this idea, with further pushing, that my classes often cling to. "Stud City" isn't about Gordie, but it is. "The first story I ever wrote that felt like *my* story," he tells us. This idea feels important—it explains why the odd-fitting short story is in "The Body" in the first place; and it is important within the larger idea of our coming of age theme. "Finding yourself," my students had answered the first week of class when asked what "coming of age" meant to them. "Becoming who you are," they'd added, echoing the idea at the very core of the pleasure of that first story you write that feels like *your* story, after trying to write like whoever you thought you were supposed to try to write like. George Saunders has talked of his own "becoming a writer origin" story, all the blue collar, dirty-realism stories he wrote because he thought that's what short stories were supposed to be. And then that story happens where you find your own voice, you realize none of your "Raymond Carver stories" were very good because you aren't Raymond Carver; something clicks into place and you write *your* story.

As parallel, maybe I should have dropped in one of my much older short stories in place of "Eulogy for Barnes and Noble #2628." Something that feels less connected to this book, but could in one way or another echo its themes of nostalgia, growing up, coming of age. The stories I've written over the years overflow with these themes, and I'm sure I could have ferreted out one as "the first story I ever wrote that felt like *my* story—the first one that really felt *whole*." And yet, "Eulogy" is the first piece of nonfiction I published, the first thing I wrote where I most explicitly attempted memoir, the first time I tried digging at some kind of history of my own story of becoming a writer that this book is continuing.

"Only slightly changed," Gordie tells us about the "Stud City" we just read, as compared to that original published in *Greenspun Review*. "I've resisted the urge to change it a lot more, to rewrite it, to juice it up." This is appealing as confession—we get to see a less refined version of Gordie through this "only slightly changed" older story, while also seeing current Gordie as more mature, able to recognize his own immaturity. More meta, it gives King the opportunity to use an old, otherwise forgotten story, while also calling himself out on being "melodramatic," "derivative," "sophomoric," and even his own story's "attitude toward women" that "goes beyond hostility and to a point which actually verges on actual ugliness." It also isn't entirely true. Indeed, King may have resisted the urge to change writing he finds "quite embarrassing now," but the story has been edited since its publication in *Ubris* in 1969 to heighten the presence of Chico's brother, Johnny, because Chico is dealing with his brother's death in the same way that Gordie himself is in "The Body." Chico's relationships with his dad and his stepmom aren't the same as the relationships that have made Gordie feel like the Invisible Boy, but there are echoes, what Charles Baxter, in his book about writing, *Burning Down the House*, calls "Rhyming Action." "Stud City" was the first story, Gordie tells us, that he never showed his parents. "There was too much Denny in it. Too much Castle Rock. And most of all, too much 1960."

After a lengthy discussion, my students usually find the inclusion of "Stud City" more interesting than they'd at first thought. It feels "true," they say, a mature view on the complications of fiction and nonfiction.

9

Only, I wasn't really twelve going on thirteen when I first saw *Stand By Me*, I don't think. I remember my parents sitting me down, giving me something of a warning, and then us watching the movie, but I don't actually remember how old I was.

My memory, in general, is kind of horrible. Possibly because of general tendencies toward allowed laziness of thought, possibly because my life has been pretty easy, my memories of growing up are almost all good. Idyllic, even. As *Anna Karenina* famously opens, "All happy families are alike, every unhappy family is unhappy in its own way." It's *possible* my life has been too boringly happy for even me to remember. Which makes those memories that I can most easily recall[19] stand out all the more for that unique distinction.

My wife often teases me, asking how I can be a writer, an *artist*, with such a happy childhood. The fucked-up childhood isn't necessarily a prerequisite to becoming an artist, but it certainly seems common, and probably helps. I laughed

---

19. See: this book, and the depth of analysis devoted to the few memories herein.

listening to Kevin Smith on the Bret Easton Ellis podcast, when he said,

> I was never like, "ohh, my childhood sucked, my teenage years sucked." I had a good time. So when people talk about, I get it, and I've read a lot of people, a lot of biographies . . . read up on cats you're interested in and shit, and you always see a long list of pain. And I feel bad, and I go, "maybe that's why my shit sucks," cause I don't have that. I'm not driven by this fuckin' demon that I'm like, I gotta beat out and shit. So, for me, I'll never be able to take it to that next immortal level . . . I don't have an ounce of pain in my background that warrants "great art." I have enough pain to get you "good enough art."

That sounds about right.

Stand By Me was released in theaters in August of 1986, so would have been released on VHS the following year. I find it easier to believe that my dad picked up the movie from a new release wall than randomly three years later, having never seen it in the interim. I also find it easier to picture my parents having the previously mentioned talk with me if I were the nine I would have been in 1987, rather than twelve. I guess I could ask them. Maybe they'd remember the year, how old I'd been, how long, at the time of that viewing, we'd lived in the house in which I grew up, the house in which the scene of my memory occurs, the house that we moved into when I was nine.

Or maybe they wouldn't. Watching *Stand By Me* for the first time wasn't an *event* in their lives. It wasn't the first time they saw something that would become the movie they've seen the most, the movie they most frequently reference and quote. Neither of my parents is currently, at least to the best of my knowledge, working on a book devoted to said movie and the novella on which it was based. Watching *Stand By Me* wasn't similar to the first time they saw an animal that would later become their favorite animal, the animal they'd read a multitude of books about, the animal that bore the name of the distillery where they got married, the animal whose name they had tattooed over their hearts.

So maybe they'd remember the year, maybe they could either correct or confirm my own memory, but probably not. And that feels less interesting anyway. What matters is the memory itself, and if there's a secondary interest, it is in my attempt at asking what year it *likely* was. Looking up when the movie came out, doing basic math to place my own age at the time. Working through if that age and timeframe makes sense. When I teach, that's what I'm asking my students to do. They've been taught how to do basic research and then to write papers essentially just to prove that they did said research. What I'm asking them to do is ask questions. Wrestle with things and try to work through some ideas for themselves. Try to let go, at least a little, of this idea of there being a right and a wrong answer, and instead discover what might be an explanation behind a question to which there isn't such a straightforward simple answer. And then make your argument.

So that's where I'm at. I was more than likely nine the first time I saw *Stand By Me*. But both the movie and the novella begin with the same line—"I was twelve going on thirteen the first time I saw a dead human being"—and so it sounds better to want to say I was twelve going on thirteen the first time I saw the movie. Not only sounds better, but *feels* better; and not only *better*, but more *right*. Like more narratively honest. Which feels like an argument probably only a writer would make, but that means it feels like one Gordie Lachance himself might make. It is, more or less, the argument "Stud City" at least implicitly makes.

Maybe I was twelve going on thirteen when I first read "The Body"?

10

Teddy and Chris and Gordie are playing cards when Vern asks if they "want to go see a dead body?" and then we get the backstory of that body, Ray Brower: a kid who lived maybe forty miles from Castle Rock, and had gone missing three days before. He'd gone out to pick blueberries and never returned, and so now, three days later, everyone was presuming he would never be found alive, maybe never found period. "We had all listened to the Ray Brower story a little more closely," Lachance tells us, "because he was a kid our age."

"Vern Tessio had been under his porch that morning, digging," the next chapter starts. "We all understood that right away, but maybe I should take just a minute to explain it to you." Vern, it turns out, was under his porch digging because, four years before, when he was eight, he'd buried a jar of pennies (i.e. "buried treasure," i.e. "*booty*") under there, and drew himself a treasure map. Only a month or so passed before he decided to dig it up ("being low on cash for a movie or something"), but in that time his mom had cleaned his room and thrown away his map. He'd tried to find the spot from memory. No luck. He'd been trying on and off ever since, but still hadn't found them. "Four years, man," Lachance interrupts his own narrative to comment. "Four *years*. Isn't that a pisser? You didn't know whether to laugh or cry."

The scene works narratively in explaining how Vern, and then all four kids, know where to find Ray Brower's body. While under the porch, Vern had overheard his brother, Billy, and Billy's friend, Charlie Hogan, talking about having discovered a body. (They, in turn, had discovered it after having stolen a car, taken their girlfriends out "parking," then going off into the woods to "take a piss by the tracks.") But it's also just a great, funny moment. Vern could have overheard his brother and Charlie under any number of circumstances, but there is something about the pennies that feels special.

Thinking about it now, I recall my own childhood fascinations with pirates, maps, *treasure*, which reminds me of another eighties' film, *Goonies*. It came out the year before *Stand By Me*, also featured a very young Corey Feldman as one of a group of four friends, and is essentially built on the premise of these kids finding a treasure map. There is something magical about treasure maps: they are specific, visual symbol for adventure; within that adventure is the allure of danger—danger to be averted and outsmarted, but also danger that holds a reward at the other end. There are secrets out there, with the possibility of endless riches, waiting to be discovered, if only you knew how to find them. If only you went looking.

If the idea of the treasure map is the fishing line being cast out into the water, the image of Vern and his pennies sets the hook. It is one of the images from *Stand By Me* that most sticks with me, and is perhaps one of the few distinct advantages of the movie over the book: the image of a hundred holes dug under a porch, so perfectly cinematic, Vern looking completely crestfallen, unable to find his buried treasure. "Four *years*."

"We ragged him about it something wicked," Lachance confesses to us. "His nickname was Penny—Penny Tessio."

The image of Vern digging for those pennies for four years and never finding them does indeed make me want to both laugh *and* cry, but maybe what I love most of all is how this singular thing represents so much of Vern as a character. It's his *thing*, for better or worse.

It feels simplistic to boil a character down to one singular thing, but simplistic doesn't mean not real. If anything, I'd argue just the opposite: it might feel less real if none of the four characters had a nickname, much less one based on something that character was probably embarrassed by. Sometimes, a singular interest can become shorthand for who we are— sometimes those things feel a little foisted upon us, and sometimes we get to decide those things ourselves. Vern's mom threw away his treasure map when he was eight, and now he's "Penny." If Vern had ever found his pennies, or even if he'd just given up, or if his mom had never thrown away his treasure map in the first place, he wouldn't have overheard his brother and Charlie talking about Ray Brower's body. An overheard story that itself then becomes something of a treasure map for the four boys' journey.

Vern, Teddy, Chris and Gordie devise a plan to tell their parents they're "campin out in Vern's back field." They then go their separate ways to tell their parents and get supplies, and we see Gordie interact with his dad. Or, not really interact. Instead, we see Gordie as ignored son, and get some more family history, about his relationship with his brother, Denny. We already know Denny died in a Jeep accident, and that, in its wake, Gordie felt like "the Invisible Boy," The next chapter is "Stud City."

In *Stand By Me*, we can't really pause to read a story Gordie wrote ten years in the future, but we do get a couple fuzzy-around-the-edges-to-signify-flashback/memory scenes of Gordie and John Cusack as Denny hanging out. Denny teasing his little brother, giving him a noogie. A scene of the two brothers and their parents sitting around a dinner table— their father keeps asking Denny about football, but Denny keeps trying to redirect the conversation to a story Gordie had written, maybe the most cinematic way to represent the inclusion of "Stud City," now that I think about it.

After "Stud City" and a chapter of reflection on the short story, we return to Gordie in his room. He collects two blankets into a bedroll, and all his money: sixty-eight cents. He then walks back toward the clubhouse and meets up with Chris. Together, they pass the Blue Point Diner, the Castle Rock Drugstore, behind which they run down an alley, where Chris shows off a pistol he'd *hawked* out of his dad's bureau. They meet up with Vern and Teddy, and Chris shows off the gun again. "We might see a bear," Chris reasons, when asked what they needed a pistol for. "Something like that. Besides, it's spooky sleeping out at night in the woods."

And, finally, their journey begins.

"We walked out of the vacant lot together, Chris slightly in the lead."

11

In July 2015, I went to *Stand By Me* Day in Brownsville, Oregon.

I had learned about it while searching online for where the movie had been filmed. I found the website of the city of Brownsville, and then a link to the Day. It's held every July 23rd, which was only a month or two away when I discovered it. It felt like fate; or, if not *fate*, at least like something I should do.

I'd actually been looking for a way to have a guy's weekend. My wife does this once or twice a year, give or take—she and a few friends fly to Miami, or Jamaica, or Myrtle Beach, and have an informal "writer's retreat." They share work, and the trip gives them a deadline to finish something, and then an opportunity to get some feedback, to talk about writing. But then, of course, it's really an excuse to hang out with friends.

So, I'd been looking to organize a retreat weekend with my friends, and here was a day devoted to the movie I was working on a book about. I was on summer break, a summer with possibly the least amount of travel planned since I'd started teaching. Plus, it was in Oregon! I love Oregon! And, probably more importantly, Brownsville was a mere drive away for most of my old friends who still lived in Tacoma and Seattle.

I got on AirBnB and found an adorable cottage, perfectly located in downtown Brownsville. I then invited both my old, college, non-writer friends, and my current, mostly-writer friends, thinking it might make for a great mashup of groups—those who I thought of as my own personal Chrises and Teddys and Verns, as well as those who might most relate to my working on a book about those same friends. I reserved the cottage for a week, and hoped only that more friends than the cottage could sleep wouldn't take me up on the offer.

I started hearing back from people. My best friend since I'd moved to Lakewood when I was nine, Brad, was going to be in California, leading a mission trip. All of my writer friends who lived anywhere but the west coast had family obligations. It was the middle of summer, it was relatively last-minute notice, they all had plans, they all had young children. (Now I understood why my wife had gone on many of her writer retreats with single women who didn't have families.) Wes, my college roommate, who I have known since junior high and who also lived with me when I moved back to Seattle before he joined the Air Force Reserve and I moved east to Michigan, rarely knew his flight schedule very far in advance and so while he wanted to come, wouldn't know for sure until the last minute.

A few of my writer friends who lived in Portland, only an hour or two north of Brownsville, thought they might be able to make the drive down, but likely only for one night, and even then it was a schedule-dependent, play-it-by-ear possibility.

My buddy Brooks had maybe the least firm conflict, but was still only a "tentative yes . . . onnacounta money and other trips we got planned."

In the end, Brooks was able to make it, as was Wes, who brought along his buddy Mark, who I'd known since high school, though we hadn't really ever hung out much. So, there were, of course, four of us.

One difference between "The Body" and *Stand By Me* are a few lines from the novella that didn't make it to the film:

"There were five, maybe six steady guys and some other wet ends who just hung around."

It makes sense that there is no mention of extraneous friends in *Stand By Me*. As a filmmaker, you want to streamline the story, focusing on the characters central to the narrative. You don't want to clutter things up with the name of a friend who was out of town, or a friend who couldn't make it.

After the boys tell their parents the false story that they'll be camping in Vern's backyard, Gordie asks, "What about John and Marty?" John and Marty DeSpain are apparently two other members of the "regular gang." Chris answers, "They're still away. . . . They won't be back until Monday."

It's throwaway information, unnecessary to the movie, but it fills out the world, and acknowledges the fluidity of the group. These four kids share the story of "The Body" not necessarily because they are the core four, but because they are the four who are hanging out when Vern shares what he's overheard about Ray Brower's body. John and Marty miss out on something that Gordie is still thinking about twenty years later, this deeply important moment in his life, probably in all four of their lives, because they happened to be out of town that weekend. That feels real.

I flew in on Monday—Detroit to Eugene, where I rented a car and drove a half an hour north to Brownsville. The town is maybe ten minutes off the freeway, and when you turn onto Main Street heading into downtown, you're immediately greeted by the bridge the four boys crossed on their way back into town at the end of *Stand By Me*. If you have seen the movie anywhere near as many times as I have, it is immediately recognizable; if you love the movie anywhere near as much as I do, it raises goose bumps up and down your arms. And then, beyond the bridge, there is the fork in the road where Teddy[20] and Vern[21] curl off from the group at the end of the movie to head to their own homes, leaving Gordie and Chris to return to the treehouse. Finally, there is a painted *Stand By Me* sign welcoming you to Brownsville, and its adorably small "historic downtown." The whole town feels timeless. It looks nearly the same today as it looks in the movie, filmed thirty years ago; and it was filmed there because thirty years ago it looked like the 1960 in which it was set.

I used my phone to guide me through downtown and to the address of the cottage. I hardly needed it though: it was two blocks from downtown, itself a stretch of barely more

20. "See you later." "Not if I see you first."
21. "Hey, look. A penny!"

than two blocks. I parked, let myself in. The place was adorably decorated.[22]

I went out to eat,[23] and again used my phone as guide, this time on a walking tour through Brownsville's *Stand By Me* locations. The tree where the treehouse was built for the filming. The Brownsville Saloon that doubled as the movie's pool hall, Irby's. Around the block, behind the bar, is the alley where Chris shows Gordie the gun he took from his dad. Back to the fork in the road and the bridge I'd driven over on my way into town.

I returned to the cottage and appreciated that I had a full day to myself before my friends got into town. I was most excited for this trip because my friends were going to share it with me, but I also enjoyed walking the town and having a meal by myself, as well as having the house to myself for the night. I thought about taking notes for this book, but realized I didn't want to. This book had instigated the trip, but wasn't really the reason I was in Brownsville. I wasn't here as *research*, but to see and hang out with friends, as journey, as adventure.

I texted my friends that I was excited for them to get here the next day. Then I read some and went to bed early.

---

22. In case I needed any final clues of fate: there were only five or six DVDs on the bookshelf, but they included *Mallrats*, one of my other favorite movies, a distinction I'll get to....
23. There is a bar downtown that serves food, and a Mexican restaurant; I had a burrito and margarita.

12

During my senior year of high school, I applied to only one college. I knew I wanted to go to the University of Washington rather than Washington State University, and the only other schools I'd heard of were from movies or college basketball, places like Yale or Harvard, Stanford or Duke, schools that rich people went to and/or whose mascots I knew from their sports' teams. I wasn't rich, and I didn't play sports, so I applied to UW. I filled out my FAFSA and went on a campus tour for families of prospective students. I filled out paperwork for dorm preference, I went on an overnight orientation for incoming students. I signed up for classes.

I didn't receive any scholarships, and got less financial aid than I'd hoped, so it was determined that I couldn't afford to live on campus. Instead, I lived at home and commuted, most days riding the bus, which took about an hour and a half each way. Still, it wasn't bad. I read, I listened to music on my Discman, I did a little homework, I napped. I didn't write, because I hadn't started writing yet, although it now occurs to me that maybe this excess downtime, pre-smartphones and other pure time-wastes, was when I really started reading.

Mostly what I remember about my freshman year was feeling like I didn't fit in at home, but I didn't fit in at college, either. My grandmother was sick and came to live with us in a house too small to hold anyone more than it already did, so my parents and my mom's siblings all pitched in and bought a camper, which was parked in our driveway. My grandmother moved into my parents' room, my parents into mine, and I lived in the camper.[24]

It was my own place, *kind of,* but it wasn't a dorm an hour away from my parents, surrounded by independence and alcohol and a community of kids in the same position as me. The computer lab became an excuse to procrastinate leaving campus to return to the camper in my parents' driveway, but it was also the first time I was ever online. We didn't have a computer at home—my grandmother had had one at her home office, before she'd moved in with us, and I'd loved whenever I was allowed to use it, but mostly just to play games and to create spreadsheets to keep track of my baseball cards.[25] Every day after classes, I would go to Odegaard Undergraduate Library, check my email on a University DOS program, and "surf the Internet." I get nostalgic, thinking using Lycos and and Altavista and Yahoo, all

---

24. A photo of which I would trace five years later for somewhat-joking use on a very early version of the *Hobart* website. That tracing then became the de facto Hobart logo: it has been on every incarnation of the website since, is on the spine of fifteen print issues of the journal, and five Hobart editors, myself and Elizabeth included, have gotten it as tattoo.

25. I would love to say I also used it to write horrible, early stories, but writing stories hadn't occurred to me by the time I was taking the bus to college; it certainly hadn't in middle and high school when I was cataloguing baseball cards and playing computer pinball.

pre-Google, and also thinking about how miniscule it all seems compared to what is available online now, but at the time it felt infinite. I spent a lot of time searching for skateboarding sites and photos of Drew Barrymore. I read the "Ain't It Cool News" movie reviews almost religiously, I became immersed in two of my favorite directors: Quentin Tarantino and Kevin Smith.[26]

Two years earlier, I'd seen *Pulp Fiction* in the theater, and it had blown my mind. I'd never seen anything like it. Like remembering sitting down in my living room to watch *Stand By Me* for the first time, seeing *Pulp Fiction* in the theater is one of my movie-going experiences I specifically remember. I was sixteen at the time, a junior in high school. It would have been the first year I could drive myself to the theater, though it likely wasn't the *first*, as the movie was released in October and I would have had my license for eight months by then, and going to the movies with friends was a common occurrence. Still, the only film I specifically recall seeing is *Pulp Fiction*.

I remember getting in my first car, my grandmother's 1986 Ford Mustang that she had given me for my sixteenth birthday, and driving to the movieplex across town, in University Place. I don't remember who I went with, but I do remember pulling into the parking lot, parking the car, seeing the movie's title on the marquee, and standing in line. I remember being *excited*, I remember it being *talked about*. Pre-Twitter, pre-"Golden Age of TV," pre-ever having had a job, much less one with a water cooler, it is perhaps the first time I remember there being such

---

26. The importance of Kevin Smith in my life feels almost worthy of deeming as "confession," maybe second after that I still haven't a *Friday the 13th* or *Nightmare on Elm Street*.

a thing as "water cooler talk." I remember that my parents had already seen it and, a little similar to *Stand By Me*, actually, now that I think about it, I remember them having their problems with it (the amount of swearing, the violence), but also raving about it—the quality of the writing, the directing.

I remember sitting in that movie theater, finally, after hearing my parents and so many other people talk about the movie. I remember the screen filling with a dictionary definition of "pulp," and that definition segueing into a couple talking in a diner, everyday chatter that seemed both mundane and hypnotic. I remember "Garçon! Coffee!"; I remember, "I love you, Pumpkin," "I love you, Honey Bunny"; I remember, "All right, everybody be cool, this is a robbery!" "Any of you fucking pricks move, and I'll execute every motherfucking last one of ya!" and then a freeze-frame, accompanied by surf guitar, and then a long list of credits over a black screen. I remember thinking, *holy shit!*

And then, two years later, I had graduated high school and was in college, where I spent a good amount of time in the computer lab. Kevin Smith and Tarantino were two of my favorites because they'd made movies unlike anything I'd seen before, movies perfectly suited to me, as they built universes perfectly timed for the emergence of the Internet.

The website of Kevin Smith's production company, View Askew, included photos, information about his films, and also the first message board I'd ever encountered, years before I found the message board for writers and editors where I met my wife. Mostly I lurked there without posting anything, baffled that I could sit in front of a computer and be carried along as one of my favorite directors posted his thoughts and responded to questions by fans. By regular guys. (Girls, too, sure; but let's be honest . . . it was most assuredly almost all guys posting on a Kevin Smith message board.) Not to mention View Askew producers like Vincent Pereira and Brian Lynch, occasionally Jason Mewes, and sometimes even Jason Lee—something of a superhero to eighteen-going-on-nineteen-year-old Aaron, as he had been a professional skateboarder and starred in one of my favorite movies, *Mallrats*.

Being online meant being able to keep track of all my favorites—Jason Lee's skateboard company, Stereo Skateboards; the much-talked-about-at-the-time *Superman Lives* script by Kevin Smith—but it also meant discovering fan theories, hidden secrets, Easter eggs. I spent a lot of time, for instance, reading about the the contents of the mysterious glowing suitcase in *Pulp Fiction,* as well as the Band-Aid on Ving Rhames' neck. In the scene at the pawnshop, there is a Killian's Red neon sign, with only "KILL ED" lit up. Later, we see Bruce Willis's character pick up Zed's keys, with a "Z" on the key ring. *Kill Zed.*

Most of that trivia didn't add to the enjoyment of either movie, but also . . . it did. Smith and Tarantino were building worlds, filled with little secrets as well as connections. John Travolta's character, Vincent Vega, was the brother of Michael Madsen's Victor Vega, aka Mr. Blonde in *Reservoir Dogs.* In *Clerks,* Dante and Randal close the store to attend Julie Dwyer's wake the day after she died in a YMCA pool, and in *Mallrats,* T.S. and Brandi break up due to Julie Dwyer's death.

This wasn't anything new, of course—I was familiar with, say, the *Star Wars* universe—but this was different. Smith's and Tarantino's worlds weren't sci fi, but were more or less our own, they were real, and since nothing in our world exists singularly, it made sense that these movie characters might know each other, might even be related. It felt like being told a secret. Its why, when going back and reading "The Body" as an adult, I love that it is set in Castle Rock, where King has set many of his stories. I love that, when the dump keeper's dog, Chopper, is first mentioned,[27] as the "most feared and least seen dog in Castle Rock," that description is later amended to "at least until Joe Camber's dog Cujo went rabid twenty years later.[28]

I also love that, when the four boys are crossing the train bridge, Gordie has something of a premonition before squatting down and putting his hand on the rail to feel and confirming, yes, a train is coming. He tells us, "And although I've since written seven books about people who can do such things as read minds and precognit the future, that was when I had my first and last psychic flash."

As a reminder:[29]

1. *Carrie* (1974): teenage girl with psychic powers
2. *'Salem's Lot* (1975): horror novel with vampires
3. *The Shining* (1976): young boy with psychic abilities
4. *The Stand* (1977): post-apocalyptic horror/fantasy
5. *The Dead Zone* (1979): man comes out of coma with psychic powers

---

27. In chapter 11, before his actual appearance at the dump scene in the next chapter.
28. *Cujo*, a psychological horror novel about a rabid dog, was Stephen King's second published novel, in 1981.
29. As previously tallied, these are the novels published by Stephen King, and so do not include the short story collection, *Night Shift* (1977), nor the novels published under the pseudonym Richard Bachman: *Rage* (1976), *The Long Walk* (1978), and *Roadwork* (1980).

6. *Firestarter* (1980): husband and wife with telepathic abilities

7. *Cujo* (1981): rabid dog

I don't actually know, without looking it up, which of the above books do or don't take place in Castle Rock. And yet, I know it is a city within the Stephen King universe. Furthermore, King is a large enough presence in pop culture for me—and I imagine most people—to know that he has written books "about people who can do such things as read minds and precognit the future." I know it, and I would bet that you know it, and I like that King is not only self-aware enough to know it as well, but that he knows that we know. While the sentence works on its own terms, giving us the information it is trying to convey, and then moving on, there's an added pleasure at counting King's books and figuring out that he is at the same seven as Gordie Lachance mentions ever briefly in passing.

13

Some semesters, I use the previously-mentioned-in-footnote Matt Bell essay, "Ken Sent Me: Lost in the Land of the Lounge Lizards," in my classes. The essay is about the adolescent Bell's learning about sex through his playing of *Leisure Suit Larry in the Land of the Lounge Lizards*, an adult-themed video game where the objective is literally to get the titular, virgin Larry to "score." I teach the essay because it is about Bell's coming of age—in our class-themed "The Rhetoric of Growing Up"—as well as an ideal pivot from our own reflective narrative section into cultural analysis.[30]

I am reminded of that essay now because of the way it opens: "I am not Leisure Suit Larry, except for when I am." "The Body" was written by Stephen King, obviously, but the narrator and protagonist, Gordon Lachance, is not only a very Stephen King-like writer himself, but one who acknowl-

---

30. I *also* teach it because, well, I edited the essay, and originally published it, in *Hobart #9: Games* (2008), and I first added it to our class readings one semester when Bell was in town doing a reading and so he came into class to talk with my students about the essay, always a nice change in pattern for students and break in lesson planning for teacher.

edges he is telling us a tale. As previously noted, both King and Lachance, at this point, have "written seven books about people who can do such things as read minds and precognit the future." Even writing about that sentence itself . . . I wrote, "He tells us, 'And although I've since written seven books. . . ,'" is the "he" Lachance or King?

Bell revisits a version of this question in his book *Baldur's Gate II*:

> It is sometimes difficult to determine correct pronouns when discussing an RPG like *Baldur's Gate II*, where Gorion's Ward—the player character—can be of variable gender, race, and occupation. Who is the character and who am I? How separate are these entities? When writing about in-game experiences, are they happening to my version of Gorion's Ward or are they happening to me, the player? What should we call the character at the heart of our story?

I am probably making it more complicated than it need be; differentiating between Lachance and King isn't really the same thing as the distinction between the "I" of player and that of character in a role-playing game. And, to some degree, my complication has only arisen because of writing this book. But I also think that complication is an undervalued element in the novella. When referring to the writing in "The Body," do I refer to it as that of King or Lachance? It's King's writing, of course, but as King writes later in the novella, "In the years between then and the writing of this memoir, I've thought remarkably little about those two days in September, at least consciously."

That Lachance is in many ways a stand-in for King doesn't feel like the cheat of an author making his narrator a writer out of laziness, so much as it gives the story a frame. One of the reasons "The Body" feels so real is because (adult) Gordie reminds us of King, who is of course real. For Lachance, this isn't just a story about growing, about the first time he saw a dead human being; it is the "true story" of his own coming of age. I think, much like Bell preparing us, "Sometimes I will say *I*, and mean either the character or me," sometimes I will say "The Body" is *by* King, and other times *by* Lachance. "There is no one right answer," Bell adds, "and all these modes have their own nuances useful for the purposes of discussing the 'role-playing' part of an RPG. . . ."

"The Body" is Stephen King's novella; and it is Gordie Lachance's memoir.

14

The four boys set out on their journey, following the train tracks out of town. Once they leave Castle Rock proper, a train comes. The boys move from the tracks to watch the train pass, except for Teddy, who wants to dodge it, recalling our introduction to him—he was "the dumbest guy we hung around with, I guess, and he was crazy," that his "big thing was what he called 'truck-dodging.'"

The boys then realize that none of them thought to bring food for their journey, so they pool their money together to buy some stuff at the store at the end of the road near the dump. Together, they have $2.37, "not bad," Gordie says, though Vern only has seven cents to add to the fund. The novella leaves it at that, but in the movie, Vern adds, "I still haven't found my pennies."

In the next chapter, the boys arrive at the Castle Rock dump, where previous chapters have told us they'd obtained the corrugated tin sheet for the roof of their clubhouse, as well as the "Philco with a cracked case" radio on which they'd heard about the story of Ray Brower. They each flip a penny to see who has to walk to the store for provisions. On first flip all get tails—a small moment, really neither here nor there for our purposes, but if you've seen the movie, you've no doubt at some point referred to some sign of bad luck as a "goocher." They flip again, and Gordie is the odd man out.

The chapter ends as Gordie "hauled out of there, giving them the finger over my shoulder as I went." But then he adds one more reflection, seemingly out of nowhere: "I never had any friends later on like the ones I had when I was twelve. Jesus, did you?" In *Stand By Me*, the line is slightly tweaked to "Jesus, does anyone?" and doesn't come here, but is the note the movie ends on, not narrated via voiceover by Richard Dreyfuss as adult-Gordie, but typed on his computer, presumably as part of his memoir, "The Body." I like the movie version slightly better, the all-encompassing "everyone" over the "you" directed specifically at the reader, but in either version, it's one of my favorite lines. The pondering, the focus on friendship, the confidence and pride that Gordie has in his own friends over anyone else's.

Gordie then goes down the road to the Florida Market. At the store, the owner asks him about his dead brother, Denny, and also tries to overcharge him for the food. Gordie returns, climbs the fence back into the dump, where the dump keeper, Milo, tries to sic his dog on Gordie. Gordie escapes, but Milo threatens to tell the boys' parents what they are doing, specifically getting Teddy riled up by calling his dad a *loony*.[31] After leaving the dump, the boys get to the train bridge—

---

31. Which, again, that second chapter had told us Teddy's dad was at the VA hospital after holding Teddy's head down cast-iron burner plates, burning both ears.

the crossing of which is the scene I still remember my dad referencing before my very first viewing of the movie—and after they successfully cross the bridge, the boys relax, and Gordie tells them his "Lard Ass" story.

That's the basic gist of those six chapters around the halfway point of the story. Despite the richness of the material, not that much happens narratively. This is one of the things my students say they like about the book—something isn't always happening; often the boys are just hanging out, quietly walking the train tracks together, and some of the joy of the story is that we get to spend time walking those tracks with them. In my classes, we talk about the pleasure of familiarity with friends, that we don't always have to be doing something when we are with them, that we don't have to fill every moment of silence. "The Body" captures that, feels real because of the simple ways it shows these friends just hanging out.

15

Another memory, half-remembered: reading *A Clockwork Orange* in high school. Except, I don't think I actually read it.

High school is when you watch *A Clockwork Orange* and it blows your mind and you and your friends call each other *droog* for a week. Then, you all try to read the book, and maybe one guy keeps at it and finishes, and proceeds to tell the rest of you it's worth it, you just gotta stick with it, it's even better and fucking crazier than the film. So you flip through the book, have some fun consulting the appendix for Burgess's made-up words, while the friend who read the book says that if you like the words, you'll love the book, just give it another try, but the rest of you have already given up and gone back to whatever it is you all talk about, back to movies, back to reading *Thrasher* and *Transworld Skateboarding*. Despite now being a reader and writer, I was one of the guys that gave up.

I don't actually remember reading anything in high school. I must have read at least a handful of books for English classes, but I don't remember what. I know I never had to read the oft-required *Catcher in the Rye*. I don't remember if we were assigned *The Great Gatsby* or not, but it felt completely new and unfamiliar when I read it when I was thirty.[32]

The one book I do remember is *A Clockwork Orange*. But not for however far into it I got before giving up, nor the appendix, other than that it existed. What I remember is the preface, where the author Anthony Burgess noted that, when the book came out in the United States, it was missing the final chapter from the version that had been released in the United Kingdom. This chapter had redeemed the protagonist, Alex: "He grows bored with violence and recognizes that human energy is better expended on creation than destruction," Burgess wrote. What I find interesting now, rereading the preface as a teacher and a writer, is that the final, deleted chapter "gives the novel the quality of genuine fiction, an art founded on the principle that human beings change." Burgess continues:

> There is, in fact, not much point in writing a novel unless you can show the possibility of moral transformation, or an increase in wisdom, operating in your chief character or characters. Even trashy bestsellers show people changing. When a fictional work fails to show change, when it merely indicates that human character is set, stony, unregenerable, then you are out of the field of the novel and into that of the fable or the allegory. The American or

---

32. I passingly remember both of the first two books so far in this Bookmarked series, *Slaughterhouse Five* and *A Separate Peace*, though nothing other than their titles and authors.

Kubrickian Orange is a fable; the British or world one is a novel.

In my writing classes, I frequently share with my students the Toni Morrison quote, "Everything I have written is a movement toward knowledge: if the main character doesn't know something extremely important at the end of the book that he or she didn't know at the beginning then it doesn't work for me. It's not like a happy ending, I don't mean that, it's not an a-ha moment, it's just that you grow and learn."

On one end of the spectrum, one of the biggest hurdles for my students can be writing *stories* rather than *anecdotes;* and on the other end, an overreliance on big twists or surprises. It's Burgess' fable versus novel, its Morrison's reminder that you "grow and learn" but that doesn't have to mean an "a-ha moment" or a happy ending.

It's something my students struggle with; it's something I've struggled with. There is the understanding of those two quotes, and then there is the struggle to implement them. Finally, too, there is the impulse to push back, to show that people don't always grow and learn.

Before rereading Burgess' preface, my hazy memory was such that the US publisher's deletion of the final chapter was, in fact, a push toward optimism. If I'd had to guess, I would have bet that Burgess' intention was to present a lack of change, to explore the idea that not everyone is redeemed, and that the publisher thought the book's audience would want a happier ending. However, this is adult/writer/teacher me thinking about character growth and morality, redemption and the marketplace's expectations thereof. What stood out at the time, and what stuck with me in the intervening two decades, was Burgess' sadness over the lost chapter changing the number of chapters in the book:

> The book I wrote is divided into three sections of seven chapters each. Take out your pocket calculator and you will find that these add up to a total of twenty-one chapters. 21 is the symbol of human maturity, or used to be, since at 21 you got the vote and assumed adult responsibility. . . . Novelists of my stamp are interested in what is called arithmology, meaning that number has to mean something in human terms when they handle it. The number of chapters is never entirely arbitrary. . . . Those twenty-one chapters were important to me.

In high school, I'd never considered that something like the number of chapters in a book mattered, that it might have been a conscious decision. Today, I encourage my students to ask these kinds of questions. *Might* something have been a conscious decision by the author? If so, what might have been the intent?

"What happens in that twenty-first chapter?" Burgess asks. "Briefly, my young thuggish protagonist grows up."

Late in the semester, my students and I look at a handful of essays that use various forms as a guide. Our *Creative Composition* calls them "borrowed forms," but also notes that Suzanne Miller and Brenda Paola, in their writing textbook *Tell It Slant,* coined the term "hermit-crab essay" for the same. A hermit-crab essay "appropriates the other forms as an outer covering to protect its soft, vulnerable underbelly." Which, in a way, is what Burgess is talking about with arithmology.

"The Body" has thirty-four chapters. "Stud City" is specifically chapter 7, with chapter 8 being devoted to "Stud City" analysis, and "The Revenge of Lard Ass Hogan" is excerpted and included as chapter 16. So that's the form I'm borrowing, the shell I am trying to hermit-crab this book into.

16

From "Items From My Childhood Which I Have Tried, but Failed, to Use As Metaphors in Stories," by Aaron Burch. Previously unpublished. Date unknown (pre-2006). Used by permission.

Speak 'N' Spell

I have thought even less about the possible greater meaning I could attribute to this wonderful toy. I don't think this could even qualify as a metaphor. What I have thought about is just how freaking cool this thing was. Carrying it by its briefcase-like handle bar, I went everywhere with my Speak N' Spell, stopping and pushing buttons to make it tell me words that I could then type out and spell correctly. I'm not sure if every kid thought this was cool as I did, or if I was just a total dork that liked to spell. I guess I could work it in somewhere as a small indicator of how much of a dork the main character in a story (me) is, but I think that usually comes across without the needed help of examples or metaphors. Also, can I work a Speak N' Spell into a story without mentioning E.T.? And then from there I would get caught up and somehow work in Reese's Pieces and then I would just want to turn it into a piece about candy in my favorite movies growing up with Baby Ruth and *Goonies* and … were there any candy bars in *Stand By Me?* Wait, Pez! Yes. "If I could only have one food for the rest of my life? That's easy. Cherry Pez. Cherry flavor Pez. There's no doubt about it." No doubt, indeed.

From "Things Go Missing," by Aaron Burch. Previously unpublished. Date unknown (pre-2006). Used by permission.

We walked along what used to be the train tracks, a path of rocks trailing down on either side of us into bushes and berry thorns. Every time we walked that path, I thought of *Stand By Me*, there always being four of us, and tried to fit each of us into the roles. I never asked for anyone else's opinion though, it being obvious Jonas would be Vern, the fat kid, and I always thought myself an asshole for knowing it was obvious.

From "Perfect," by Aaron Burch. Originally published in Phoebe *37.1, Spring 2008. Used by permission.*

Without work to go to, I went home, put in *Stand By Me*, and got in bed to sleep off the rest of my hangover. I thought about calling the dentist. I thought about all of the nights I considered flossing but didn't. Nights I'd gone to sleep without brushing, having drunk too much, or being too tired, or just too lazy. One night wouldn't make a difference, I always assured myself. What's one night, here and there? Fifteen minutes into the movie, as the boys are just heading out of town, I fell asleep.

(. . .)

All day I watched *Stand By Me*, fell asleep, started it over again from where I thought I'd left off, fell asleep again. I didn't remember any of my dreams. When I finally watched it all the way through, I just lay in bed, not really tired but not at all wanting to get up. The phone rang and I picked it up without thinking about it, just wanting the ringing to stop, not even thinking to say hello.

From Wolfmen, *by Aaron Burch. Previously unpublished, 2011. Used by permission.*

The barman put down a shot glass in front of each of us. He cracked open two beers at once, one in each hand, and placed them behind the shots. "Not you, man," Jeff clarified, and then his big, kinda-but-not-quite goofy smile. At first I thought he was nervous or covering for himself, trying to sell the bartender that he meant no offense, but then I recognized the expression from a few times earlier on the trip and realized he was just happy, showing joy and gratitude for the bar in general, the drinks in front of him and a good bartender, specifically. And then, for no reason that seemed obvious, I further realized where and why that smile of his had seemed familiar—it was the part-innocent, part-vulnerable, part-badass smile of Chris Chambers, River Phoenix, in *Stand By Me*. I thought of Benjamin and wondered what had happened to him, and realized I wouldn't be too surprised to hear he'd been killed when, trying to break up a fight, he was on the wrong end of someone pulling a knife and got stabbed in the throat. Possibly, I thought, in a bar not too unlike this one. How my life might have been different if there'd been four of us instead of just me and Benjamin. If we'd gone looking for, and found, a dead Ray Brower. I could feel my eyes starting to wet, and tried to rub them dry in a way that least made it seem like I was rubbing away the beginnings of tears.

"Maybe you're going to the wrong bars," the barman said.

"Maybe," Jeff answered. "That's possible."

The barman walked away, to ask if the guy sitting at the other end of the bar needed anything, or to chat with his regular, or just to get away from us. I pulled my attention back to Jeff, saw him with his shot raised, waiting for me. I picked up mine, went to cheers.

"What are we cheering?" Jeff asked, pulling his shot away.

"I don't know." Jeff stared at me, waiting for me to know. "Being on the road?"

"Road trips," Jeff repeated. "Road trips and beer backs. Dying arts."

I nodded, went to cheers again, but Jeff didn't move, held his glass back and away.

"One more," he said. "How about one more. I like threes. Anything?"

I thought about it, said the only thing I could think of. "*Stand By Me?*"

"Fuckin' a," he said, and smiled that River Phoenix grin, like he knew what I was thinking. "I forgot the secret knock," he said. "C'mon guys, it's me. Let me in."

"Vern!" we both said, in unison.

(. . .)

I zoned out, back in. The guy was talking, presumably answering Jeff's questions, but I was too busy thinking that if Jeff were Chris Chambers, then I was probably Gordie, and Benjamin would have been Teddy Duchamp, then who in my life had been Vern? Or maybe Benjamin would have been Chris and current, bulky Jeff was Vern. What if Jeff had hung out with me and Benjamin when we were little, or what if Benjamin and his family had stayed in town and we'd grown up together and he was on this trip with me, with us, now? Of the four, Corey Feldman seemed the most obvious choice to grow up and become a Wolfman, which would confirm Benjamin as Teddy, and Jeff as either Chris or Vern. And then there was another guy sitting across the bench from us, next to the first guy who was still talking, but this new guy wasn't listening, but also wasn't fading in and out of paying attention, like me. He was staring at Jeff with a singly-focused, drunken, how-long-is-he-going-to-hold-that stare.

(. . .)

We walked for a good hour, at least. Without my phone, and Jeff either likewise without one or still refusing to show if he had one, neither of us with a watch, and no Sunny to check the dash, we had no timepiece to consult. We stopped once and bought a couple bottles of water, some beef jerky, a handful of power and protein and granola bars. I tucked the sleeping bag I'd grabbed from Sunny before whispering my farewell under my broken hand, or held it with my right, or swung it around by its pull string, and wished the string was long enough to throw over my shoulder and carry it that way, *Stand By Me* style. Jeff had no sleeping bag and walked only with his backpack.

From "Fire in the Sky," by Aaron Burch. Originally published in The Los Angeles Review, vol. 7, spring 2010. (Collected in Backswing [Queen's Ferry Press, 2014].) Used by permission.

I'd planned to do the whole Yellowstone experience—hike the trails, see Old Faithful, watch for and count as many elk as I could find—but soon as I saw the herds of buffalo, I was hypnotized. I both wished I had someone there to share it with and was glad to be by myself and not have to share anything. I kind of wanted to take a picture and send it to my ex, show her that I was finally on the road, out seeing our country. I thought of that scene in *Stand By Me*, my favorite movie growing up, when Gordie sees the deer by the train tracks early in the morning before his buddies wake up. Narrating the movie, adult Gordie says he never did tell anyone about that deer, that he kept it as something special that only he had.

I spent two days driving around the park, sitting on my car and just watching those buffalo, daydreaming, not thinking or worrying about anything or anyone else.

From The Year of the Buffalo by Aaron Burch. Previously unpublished, 2016. Used by permission.

This was her third year showing *Stand By Me*, her fourth year teaching Stephen King's "The Body." Three years, three-to-five times a year, depending on her class schedule, not to mention all her own viewings, pre-teaching. She had it memorized, and still she more often than not noticed something she previously hadn't, or surprised herself recalling a new memory she wasn't prepared for.

On the TV, teenaged Gordie, Wil Wheaton, watches a deer near the train tracks, first thing in the morning, while adult Gordie, Richard Dreyfuss, tells us that he never told his buddies that he saw the deer. It's one of Holly's favorite scenes, though she never especially tried to understand why. I just like it—the kind of answer she'd never let her students get away with, but sometimes that's what it was. Every year she liked to ask her classes what it meant, what the deer stood for, why the scene was included in the book and movie at all. She liked asking, and liked hearing attempts at answer, both the usual and the one or two that would completely surprise her every year. She would end the class by smiling and shrugging her shoulders, "I don't know either," she'd say, but all those ideas seem smart, interesting. Something to think about, she'd leave them with.

This year, a text waiting for her on the phone she was trying not to think of; her husband at his own job, having put in his notice and so already having practically given up; a video game in the works, starring her husband, Mr. Bison, and his pet buffalo. The scene with Gordie and the deer reminded Holly of her and Scott's trip to the Badlands, sitting in his car together, and then on the hood, leaning back into windshield, holding hands, like they thought they were in a movie or something. Just watching the buffalo. How hypnotic they were. They had each other, and they talked about the buffalo, both at the moment and over the years, and she'd tell any friend who would listen when returning home from the trip, but the two scenes felt reminiscent regardless. She'd never before made the connection though, and for a brief moment she wondered if she loved the scene in *Stand By Me* because it had reminded her, albeit unconsciously, of watching buffalo in the Badlands with Scott, or vice versa, or if they were unrelated but just touched the same nerve.

17

After the train bridge scene, the boys relax and recompose themselves. "Hey, tell that story," Chris says. "What story?" Gordie answers, "although I guess I knew." Following some back and forth between the four boys, Gordie says, "Hey, I didn't even write it down yet." Gordie then starts telling the story, but Vern and Teddy keep interrupting him. When he finally gets into a rhythm and the interruptions stop, the chapter ends, "So, dig it, they come up onto the platform...."

The next chapter, chapter sixteen, begins like chapter seven's "Stud City":

From *The Revenge of Lard Ass Hogan*, by Gordon Lachance. Originally published in *Cavalier* magazine, March, 1975. Used by permission.

Published in 1975 means five years later than "Stud City," and fifteen years after Gordie's "I didn't even write it down yet" telling to his friends in 1960. The excerpt begins by repeating where Gordie had left off: "They came up onto the platform...."

"Lard Ass" is a fairly juvenile story, though differently so than "Stud City." Through Gordie's own admission, "Stud City" was "the work of a young man every bit as insecure as he was inexperienced." "Lard Ass," by contrast, is humorously immature. It may have been published five years later, when Gordie was twenty-eight rather than the twenty-three of "Stud City," but because of "The Body" we know it was a story he first told when he was only twelve.

"The Revenge of Lard Ass Hogan" is about "this fat kid nobody likes named Davie Hogan." The small town Davie lives in has an annual pie-eating contest, and Davie decides he is going to compete. However, "Lard Ass had no hope or intention of winning." As evidenced from the title, "revenge was the only blue ribbon he sought." We discover that Davie drank castor oil before the contest.[33] During the contest itself, Davie imagines the pies variously as "cowflops," "gopher guts," and "diced-up woodchuck intestines with blueberry sauce poured over them. *Rancid* blueberry sauce." These thoughts— along with the castor oil—lead to puke "roar[ing] out of his mouth in huge blue-and-yellow glurt, warm and gaily streaming," all over the contestant next to him, Bill Travis. Witnessing this leads the contest announcer to puke all over the mayor's wife, who in turn throws up on the woman next to her, and then, like dominos, everyone in the audience is throwing up on everyone else. "Lard Ass Hogan watched it all, his large face calm and beaming." And then, one of my favorite lines, in *Stand By Me* only: "A complete, and total, barf-o-rama."

In his book, *The Stephen King Story*, George Beahm writes

---

33. In *Stand By Me*, he's also shown eating a raw egg.

of "The Body": "Of King's work, this is his all-time favorite, as he said at the 1989 Pasadena lecture."[34] Beahm agrees, calling it "one of King's finest works," but with a caveat: "which to my mind would be strengthened if the two pieces of fiction within the work—stories within the main story—were deleted." Granted, both stories feel a little out of place, are not as strong or as well written as the main story around them, and neither could stand on its own. So, I see what Beahm is saying, but I disagree; I think they contribute more to the novella than may at first be obvious. Like "Stud City," "The Revenge of Lard Ass Hogan" is classic "showing" rather than "telling." It would be one thing for King to write that Gordie grew up and, fifteen years later, published a story he had told to his buddies around the campfire. However, it feels more meaningful to actually show it, which demonstrates how important this *twelve going on thirteen* summer adventure to see a dead body for a first time really was. It was so important that even the ancillary story Gordie told his friends to amuse them stuck with him enough to write and publish a decade and a half later. *A long time ago . . . although sometimes it doesn't seem that long to me.*

34. Beahm's book, however, was published in 1991, so it is entirely possible King has either changed his mind since then, or written newer "all-time favorite"'s in the twenty-five years hence.

18

A discussion that frequently arises when we're reading "The Body" in my classes is the age of the kids in the novella. My students often forget that the narrator explicitly tells us the four boys are "twelve going on thirteen," so there's always some uncertainty about how old they truly are.[35] And, even when they do remember the kids' ages, my students sometimes feel like they act older, or younger.

My students say this like they weren't "twelve going on thirteen" only a few years before.

They say it like everything they do fits within the expectations of their own age range, nineteen going on twenty, give or take a year.

They say it like they all fit within the same general con sensus understanding of "nineteen going on twenty."

We tend to make excuses for the things we like, and pick apart the tiniest inconsistencies of the things we don't. "As

---

35. And they aren't obsessed enough about the story to be writing a book about it, to devote entire chapters to that "twelve going on thirteen" sentence construction.

a critic, I recognize the significant flaws, I do," Roxane Gay pauses midway through her essay, "What We Hunger For," to confess. "But *The Hunger Games* was not a movie I am able to watch as a critic. The story means too much to me."

Maybe highlighting their disagreement of King's portrayal of "twelve going on thirteen" is my students' way of saying that they don't really like the novella. Or maybe they do like it, but they understand that discussing something in an academic setting means being critical, and this question only arises because they aren't sure what else to question. Or maybe it doesn't mean any of that, and it's just an inconsistency in their thinking. Like twelve year olds, like *all people*, aren't constantly being inconsistent.

I'm reminded of this Molly Lambert observation, writing about the TV show *Girls* for the sports and pop culture website *Grantland*.[36] Lambert cedes, "So yes, Adam has had a remarkable journey from Guy Who Takes the Condom Off Without Telling You to Guy Who Tells You That You're Beautiful, Smart, and a Great Friend. But that seemed very realish to me, because most people are nothing if not inconsistent."

There can be a tendency to object to a character's "inconsistencies" as making that character less believable, or as an example of poor writing, of having a character do whatever fits the narrative. However, a character that always does exactly as expected is considered one-dimensional, cliché, stock. Real people contradict themselves all the time. We're always doing things out of character.

---

36. RIP.

19

When my collection of stories, *Backswing*, came out in 2014, my wife interviewed me for *Hobart*.[37] One of her questions went as follows: "You say you don't have any interest in what Scott McClanahan and I somewhat jokingly (but mostly seriously) refer to as 'bleeding on the page.' Why is that? Do you think you can be a successful writer without bleeding? Is this really just a comment about your wife's writing?" In part, my lack of interest in "bleeding" was a response to my wife's writing, as it can be hard being married to an author whose writing is very personal. It also, however, is a matter of taste.

I don't read much nonfiction, and I don't especially have an interest in memoir. Nor do I really write nonfiction. Outside of school and homework, I've only written three pieces of nonfiction—one is included as a chapter in this book, and the other two were composed as humor pieces for readings.

I don't read much nonfiction, and I don't especially have an interest in memoir. Yet here is this book about "The Body" that is all nonfiction, and at least part memoir. It's like I'm telling

---

37. "Elizabeth Ellen Calls Aaron Burch On All His Shit."

you within this book I am writing that I personally wouldn't be interested in this book. So why should you be interested? I don't know. Maybe you shouldn't be.

This is how I answered my wife's question:

> I actually knew you were gonna ask something like this, and so I was thinking about it. Yes, of course, to some degree, if the artist hasn't "bled on the page" it probably can't be great art. Probably my favorite piece of art from the last decade is *Synecdoche, New York*, and Charlie Kaufman bled all over the screen in that, right? I'm thinking here of the word "confessional" and that movie is super "confessional," (right?) but that's not one of the first words you'd go to for description, I don't think. I think, sometimes, "bleeding on the page" is just that, a bunch of blood splattered on the page, and is sometimes left at that, which is fine, whatever, it's just less my thing. I'm not that into confession. I more want it crafted into more of a narrative.

When I started reading more voraciously, one of the first authors I stumbled into was Jonathan Ames. At first, via his essay collection *What's Not to Love*, though his book that has most stuck with me is his novel, *Wake Up, Sir!* Like much of Ames' writing, the narrator in the novel is a very Jonathan Ames-like character, and the setting is what I assume to be a very Yaddo-like artist colony in Saratoga Springs, New York. I assume Ames has been to Yaddo; maybe he even wrote part of *Wake Up, Sir!* there. That said, not only do I not really care if he did or didn't write it there, but I kind of don't want to know.

I like assuming that he has, but not knowing. And what really makes the novel so funny and pleasurable to me is Ames' relationship with Jeeves, a personal valet I can only assume did not accompany him to any of the stays at Yaddo I assume did occur.

In the past few years, there has been something of a movement away from the classic form of the novel, and toward work that blurs the form's edges: fiction that feels closer to real life, or even abandons fiction altogether for a novelistic nonfiction. Maybe "a movement" is too grand a term; maybe it's a topic of conversation among a small group of people who venn diagram with my life in a way that makes conversation seem like a movement. I've been a spectator to several conversations in which smart readers claim they don't care about fiction like they used to— they can't tolerate the artifice; the form feels outmoded, not representative of our time.

I'm not advocating for one over the other, only that I personally don't really want to read novels that are trying to get as close to "actual" life as possible. I am a sucker for when I can see the memoir beneath the artifice, but I'm not that interested in fiction that is thinly veiled memoir. I *like* the artifice. One could argue that Kaufman bled on the screen for *Synecdoche, New York*, but there is as much artifice as blood on the film. What I really like about *Wake Up, Sir!* is the play between the likely "true" stories of Yaddo and the more ridiculous existence of Ames being there with a valet.

One of my favorite novels, Salvador Plascencia's *The People of Paper*, is about a fictional character named Sal Plascencia who is writing a novel titled *The People of Paper*, while a student at Syracuse. While I know that Plascencia got his MFA at Syracuse, the novel is also about a woman literally made of paper, and the characters being at war with Saturn. Coincidentally, another of my favorite books of the last decade or so is by Sal's Syracuse MFA-mate, Adam Levin. I know one of Levin's teachers was Arthur Flowers, and so when a character named Flowers in *The Instructions* gives the young protagonist, Gurion, a mini-lesson on the Lauryn Hill lyric in "Zealots," I assume it was based on an actual conversation Levin had with real world Flowers, though maybe it wasn't. The scene continues with Gurion telling Flowers that his writing voice is lofty, "Because it's scripture." It's a metaphor for the very book Levin was working on, *obviously*, and I bet Levin thought, in a way that writers generally aren't supposed to have the hubris to admit, that he was trying to write a great book, capital-G great, maybe even, but I don't think he literally thought he was writing "capital-S scripture."

I guess all this is a long way of saying that I like meta-fiction, and not just because it's playful, or clever. I like the friction between "pulled from real life" and "totally fabricated," between what is obviously made-up and what the narrative not only hints toward but all but spells out *actually happened*. Most of my favorite art fits in this category. It's pointing you toward the crack in the seam, and showing you that there is beautiful art inside there.

Or maybe, most simply, it is, as Stephen King writes in the epigraph[38] to *Different Seasons:* "It is the tale, not he who tells it."

---

38. Although left credit-less at the beginning of the book, the epigraph is in fact from the final novella in *Different Seasons*, "The Breathing Method."

20

The boys walk the tracks for a bit, telling stories and hanging out, until they find a spot to camp out for the night. In the middle of the night they hear noises, leading to each of them taking a turn staying awake and keeping watch, armed with Chris's gun, which he'd "hawked" from his dad's bureau.

The next morning is possibly my favorite moment of the book and movie.

Gordie is the first to wake. He gets up, walks a few feet from his sleeping friends to piss, and then keeps on going to the railroad tracks, where he sits down. "In no hurry to wake others," he tells us. "At that precise moment the new day felt too good to share."

On the surface, "The Body" is about four boys going to see a dead body, but, of course, the dead body doesn't really matter. The book is *really* about the boys' friendship, their interactions *on the way* to see a dead body. But, here in the middle of that journey, Gordie pauses to hold onto a moment, just for himself. The sun rises, the noise of crickets begins to drop away, the birds begin to twitter. Morning *happens* and it's all Gordie's to enjoy alone.

Gordie sits there for a while, and then, just as he is about to get up, he looks to his right and sees a deer. "My heart went up into my throat," he says. He describes the deer, and then this line, "What I was seeing was some sort of gift, something given with a carelessness that was appalling."

Gordie and the deer watch each other for a little while longer, until, finally, she turns and wanders off. That's it. Gordie returns to his friends, who are all now awake. "It was on the tip of my tongue to tell them about the deer, but I ended up not doing it," he tells us. "That was one thing I kept to myself. I've never spoken or written of it until just now, today."

In the grand scheme of the story, this episode barely means much, if anything at all. While it may be an unimportant moment to the narrative, however, it is important on its own terms for the simple honesty it evokes, an honesty that is heightened by the confession that Gordie has "never spoken or written of it," until the now of the story we are reading. If he's telling us now, but has never spoken of it before, there's a newfound layer of confession to "The Body," of honesty. We're being told something new; we're being allowed in.

21

"*I was twelve going on thirteen . . .*" are the first words said, in voiceover, in *Stand By Me*, but they open the second paragraph of "The Body." The first sentence of the novella is actually, "*The most important things are the hardest things to say.*" This is something I've struggled with my whole life, not saying important things because they seemed too difficult. How much that relates to King's novella, or if it's just me digging for relatability, for pathos, I don't know. Admitting this about myself feels itself important and hard to say, so perhaps there is something there. Maybe it's the awareness and acknowledgment of this that is the true secret behind "The Body." There's the nostalgia and friendship, of course, the story's *coming of ageness*, but at the heart of "The Body" is the narrator, Gordie Lachance, confessing that *the most important things are the hardest to say*.

I have been working on this book throughout possibly the most difficult year of my marriage. I moved out of the house I shared with my wife, and we went through a couple of periods of not talking to one another, and other times when our conversations were about divorce, of the logistics of post-divorce lives. The two—"The Body," my marriage—aren't necessarily related, but they are the two things I have spent the past year contemplating. *What is "The Body" about? Should my wife and I get divorced?*

During earlier drafts of this book, one chapter began "Marriage is hard." At another point, when thinking about nostalgia, I developed a horribly reductive theory that, if we ended up getting divorced, it could be described as my wife's nostalgia for a guy we already broke up over once, before we were married; *or,* our problems could be defined as *my* nostalgia for some previous version of us as a couple, and because of this nostalgia, I didn't put in the work on us *now,* much less working toward the us in the future.

Now, however, I think I've returned to this phrase—*Marriage is hard*—just to say it here, on the page. I've found myself saying it to friends over the past year, to give language to my frustrations, voice to my struggles. It's easier for me to put on a brave face and not talk about my marriage, and bear the weight of my troubles myself. But every now and then, *marriage is hard* sneaks its way out of my mouth, along with a sigh and a half-pleading, half-weary face that asks "right?" As hard as it was to say, it has felt good saying it. Even better, it was nearly always met with agreement. *Yes,* friends would answer. *It* is *hard.* This agreement made me feel less alone. That's how art is supposed to make us feel, right? Like we're not alone? That's why sometimes it is important to say the hardest things—and, perhaps, a clue that if something is so hard to say, it might be among the most important things?

22

A chapter of the novel I am currently working on[39] begins, "I was twenty-four going on twenty-five the first time I saw a buffalo." *Twenty-four going on twenty-five* because I can't get away from that sentence construction, and also because I thought I myself was twenty-four going on twenty-five when I first saw a buffalo. Writing works by consuming everything around you, and I'd been thinking about buffalo, so I gave the observation to one of my characters, let her age be my age. Only, like my "when I first saw *Stand By Me*" claim, I'm uncertain of my own assertion here. Was it really the *first time* I saw a buffalo? It was the first time I remember. The first time I saw a buffalo and it meant something to me. Furthermore, if I actually trace my timeline backwards and do the math, I discover that's not the case.

My college girlfriend and I broke up early in 2002. I can pinpoint that year and thus begin my chronology there because we were still together and in that house in Oakland on 9/11. We broke up and I moved to southern California, where I lived

---

39. Albeit a chapter I think is going to be cut, ultimately.

by myself for a year before returning to Seattle. So now we're in early 2003, I'm chatting with a girl online who lives in "the state shaped like a mitten,"[40] then we're talking on the phone, and then she flies to Seattle to visit me, and then I fly to Michigan to visit her—the first time I'd been east of Las Vegas—and then we trade off visiting one another for the next year, and then it's mid-2004 and my roommate joins the Air Force Reserve and I store a lot of my shit in my parents' much-bigger, moved-into-after-I'd-left-the-house house, pack as much of the rest as I can fit into my Ford Escort, and hit the road. I drive south, camping my way from Seattle to Los Angeles. I climb over rocks and play in tide pools down the Oregon coast; I camp in the Redwoods, eat a "lumberjack-style" meal in Samoa, California, sleep in my tent in campgrounds, sleep in my car in church parking lots, see friends in Oakland and Sacramento and the Valley, and then cut east to Vegas, where I meet the girl I am moving to Michigan for and with. We end up in Ann Arbor, in a small apartment by the mall, with her eight-year-old daughter, and every other weekend or so, her daughter's eleven-year-old half-sister. The next summer, the four of us take a road trip across the country to Tacoma to visit my parents. Along the way we stop at the Spam Museum in Minnesota and the Corn Palace in South Dakota. We visit Mount Rushmore, we go to a rodeo in Cody, Wyoming, we camp in Yellowstone and the Badlands.

The Badlands are unlike anywhere I've ever been, like you're on the moon or another planet. And though Old Faithful in Yellowstone is cool, if a little anticlimactic, the rest of the park is as awe-inspiring as one would imagine. But what

40. Which, at the time, meant nothing to me.

I remember most about both the Badlands and Yellowstone are the buffalo. If I'd seen any before, I didn't recall. If I'd seen any before, it would have probably been in a zoo, not roaming in a herd and crossing the road and making everyone driving through the park stop and wait, not looking at once both menacing and sensitive, both massive and gentle. I remember just staring, feeling like I could watch them all day. Right now, writing this and picturing the memory, I'm remembering that moment in my life, and also this scene in the otherwise relatively forgettable *Into the Wonder* where Ben Affleck and Rachel McAdams stand on a car surrounded by buffalo, and because it is a Terrance Malick movie, it is beautiful, and because they are buffalo, it feels perfect.

I didn't make the connection back then, but every time I've watched *Stand By Me* since, every time I've reread "The Body," when I get to the part where Gordie sees a deer, I think of that road trip, and watching those buffalo. "I was about to get up when I looked to my right and saw a deer standing in the railroad bed not ten yards from me," adult Gordie writes.

> My heart went up into my throat so high that I think I could have put my hand in my mouth and touched it . . . I didn't move. I couldn't have moved if I had wanted to . . . What I was seeing was some sort of gift, something given with a carelessness that was appalling . . . We looked at each other for a long time . . . I *think* it was a long time.

I remember my own version of Gordie's moment watching the deer because it seemed like, as he put it, "I was seeing some sort of gift." I remember it because, like "The Body" represented Gordie's coming of age, that road trip represented one of my own. Only a few paragraphs ago, I said I "moved across the country for a girl," but of course I should probably say "for a woman." "Girl" feels diminutive and even a little wrong, but if I say woman, that extrapolates out to thinking of myself as a man, and I don't think I really was yet. Not when I'd moved to Michigan, although maybe by the time of that road trip. I was driving across the country with a family of my own, from my new home to my old one. Buffalo would become not just my animal, but *ours*. Years later, my future wife and I would break up, and to "win me back," she would drive to Buffalo, New York, to get a tattoo of a cave drawing of a buffalo. A couple of years after that, we'd get married in Frankfort, Kentucky, at the Buffalo Trace distillery, and another couple of years after that, I would get my own buffalo tattoo, just the word—"buffalo"—over my heart.

That drive across the country feels like the beginning of all that, the moment of transition, where there becomes a distinct before and after. When I first saw a buffalo. I feel like I was a kid, *becoming* an adult. I was twenty-seven. *Going on* twenty-eight.

23

Yesterday—the yesterday of my present, the day before I wrote the rough draft of these sentences—we talked about "charac ter" in my Introductory Creative Writing class. The textbook that I'm using this semester, Janet Burroway's *Imaginative Writing*, says, "You will have the makings of a character when you can fill out this sentence:"

(name) is a (adj.) ____-year-old (noun) who wants

_____.

I had never seen character so simply distilled before, which was helpful to me, as both writer and teacher, as well as being helpful for our class, to give us a common equation to try to figure out together. One short sentence with five fill-in-the-blanks and you have a pretty full idea of who the character is, and by extension, what the story is going to be about. We did this exercise for characters in the stories we'd read for the day's class,[41] and then—in part because I talk about pop

---

41. Tobias Wolff's "Bullet in the Brain," Jess Walter's "Anything Helps," Amelia Gray's "These Are Our Fables," and Aimee Bender's "The Rememberer."

culture as much as writing in my classes—we tried to do it for some celebrities.[42]

Then, a day later, *today*, when working on this manuscript, I thought of connecting my own experiences watching buffalo to Gordie watching the deer. And I remembered that (fictionalized) version I'd already written for the novel-in-progress I'm currently taking a break from to write this book. "I was twenty-four going on twenty-five when I first saw a buffalo."

I was x going on x+1 when I first saw (blank).

I apparently can't get away from, or let go of, this sentence structure. Echoing my feelings about "The Body," as well as Burroway's adjective/noun/desire Mad Lib, this construction tells you that I'm going to be talking about buffalo. Or *Stand By Me*. Or Gordie seeing a dead body. It tells you not only that these things will be *a* topic of conversation, but possibly *the* topic. They are important. They hold significance. We remember not just those moments of first viewing, but also the greater and surrounding moments in our lives. Further, that these moments happened in a transitional phase, possibly even during the event of transition. There was me pre-seeing a buffalo for the first time and me post; me before I'd ever seen *Stand By Me* and me after; the innocent Gordie who had never seen a dead human being, and the Gordie of after, who grew up to be a successful horror writer, who is writing and telling us the story of "The Body." Gordie, who is twelve *going on* thirteen; I, who thought I was the same, but was actually nine

---

42. Kanye, Taylor Swift, Clint Eastwood.

going on ten. I saw a buffalo. Gordie saw a dead body. I saw *Stand By Me.* Twenty-four *going on* twenty-five. Or, twenty-seven. *Going on* twenty-eight.

24

A few months ago, after having a few beers downtown, I was walking back to the apartment I'd moved into after leaving the house I'd shared with my wife. It was sometime after midnight as I crossed a small bridge over a small river that runs through town. I don't know why, but I stopped halfway across, leaned on the railing, and looked out at the water.

If I were to be totally honest, I think my subconscious reason for doing this was because it might look or sound cool. If someone walked by and saw me at that moment, they'd have seen the silhouette of someone staring fondly into the river. And if I were to replay the night later, something I was already starting to rough-draft in my mind, it would sound like a good story. *Walden*-like, maybe, with myself as an appreciator of nature, being fully in the moment, when, in fact, it was the idea of capturing the moment that had created the moment itself.

I think, here, of the easy complaints of social media. Of Facebooking or Tweeting something just so people know you are doing it. Of the admittedly annoying and obnoxious spread of, and overreliance on, digital photography, of creating and staging moments not for their enjoyment, but so that you can show off that enjoyment. Of doing something purely for the projection of that thing to others, rather than for the experience itself.

Back in high school, I vividly remember this small moment of a friend describing someone to me as "trendy."

"What do you mean?" I asked, knowing from his tone that he was being critical.

"You know. She . . . just follows whatever is trendy. Whatever is cool."

I was confused. How was that a bad thing? I would never have been accused of being trendy because I never knew what was cool in the first place. Or, on the rare occasion when I thought I might know, I didn't have the confidence to try it for myself. To try and fail at being cool seemed even worse than just being uncool.

"Why is that bad?" I asked. "Isn't everyone trying to be cool?"

It wasn't that she *is* cool, he explained. "She just jumps from one thing to the next. She doesn't think for herself."

At the time, I barely understood what my friend meant. But then I got a little older, a little more mature, perhaps; a *tiny bit* more self-confident. I started skating, listening to hardcore music, going to shows. I grew my hair long. I not only now understood what being a poseur was, but I, too, looked down on the offense. Of course, I wouldn't have considered any piece of my own identity a pose, but it had certainly started as one. Those high school complaints about being a poseur feel the same as the current knocks on Instagram or whatever: literally *posing* instead of projecting the truth.

I'm further reminded of the time my wife and I saw a live *This American Life* event. The entire show was Ira Glass, on stage alone, either walking around, or sitting behind a desk with a mixing board, like we were watching him at work, producing an episode.

The entire NPR-listening and -loving audience was enamored from beginning to end. They laughed at all the right places, leaned forward on the edges of their seats, audibly "mmmhmm'ed" at points they agreed with. I thought I loved *TAL* as much as the next college-town, theater-attending audience member, but there was something about being able to *see* Glass pushing his hands forward, raising the level of the background score as he worked toward the climactic moments of his stories, that felt like cheating.

When people are suspicious of nostalgia in art, it is usually for this reason. It can feel like cheating. It is, as Don Draper admits, "delicate but potent." Re-watching that *Mad Men* "Carousel" scene by itself, outside of the context of the surrounding episode, much less the full season leading up to it, it is easier to notice the manipulation. It's a well-written, beautifully directed, strongly-acted scene, everything working in concert to tug on and twist your emotions. The soundtrack swells, and it feels like you can literally see your strings being tugged, like a self-aware puppet.

Aware of the manipulation, *This American Life*'s storytelling spell on me broke. I left that live show feeling cold, and I didn't listen to an episode on the radio for at least a year. And yet, for whatever reason, my awareness of the puppet strings the "Carousel" scene is using on me doesn't cut me free from them. Watching it now, I feel emotional, choked up.

This American Life and *Mad Men* are using the same means toward the same ends, yet I don't ask or expect for the latter to be authentic in the way I do the former. I'm not always sure where that line is, why something falls on one side of it, and something else the other. I know the art that I most enjoy, others sometimes criticize for this very reason; while I also know I'm as guilty for being quick to put something down for this very reason.

To various degrees, we distrust artifice, nostalgia, cheating, disingenuousness. Not embracing who you are because you're trying to be something or someone else; not embracing the present because you're too focused on the past, and through rose-colored glasses, no less. "Remembrance of things past is not necessarily the remembrance of things as they were," Proust wrote. But sometimes thinking about the past can help remind you of the wonders of now. Sometimes you need to try to be someone else to figure out who you are. Sometimes staging a moment is what leads to something special. Sometimes writing about a TV show, or a movie, or a book, is the most honest way to write about yourself.

25

In that scene in the novel *The Instructions* that made me wonder if it really happened, Flowers asks Gurion his favorite rhyme in the Fugees' song "Zealots."

"My favorite's when Pras goes, 'And for you bitin' zealots, your rap styles are relics. No matter who you damage, you're still a false prophet,'" Gurion answers.

"See," Flowers responds, "that's the wrong one." A few pages later, he tells Gurion, "You ain't paid enough attention to the girl." Flowers hits play and Lauryn Hill raps, "Even after all my logic and my theory, I add a motherfucka so you ign'ant niggas hear me." Later on, Flowers tells Gurion why he'd played him that rhyme: "You got more than enough logic and theory, we both know that, but what is your motherfucker?"

I think about that section of *The Instructions* often. Like trading in a *thesis* for a *driving question*, like boiling a character down to adjective/noun/desire, it really affected me. The simplicity; the way it put into words something I already knew but hadn't put into words myself. In a way, the genre fiction complaint about literary fiction could be oversimplified into "all logic and theory, no motherfucker"; and vice versa.

When I teach, I've gotten better at allowing myself my pop culture references, my digressions about growing up or my own writing, as my *motherfucker*. In life, I find myself listening to, watching, and talking about podcasts, TV shows, sports, and standup comedy as much as, if not often more than, writing, and so I use and talk about the same in the classroom. On a recent episode of the podcast *The Moment*, Brian Koppelman talked to Mary Karr about a Thelonius Monk quote, "A genius is the one most like himself." I have found that the more "like myself" I become in the classroom, the more effective I am as a teacher. Without these asides, my class can slip into all logic and theory, my students getting as bored as I do.

In general, there are usually two reasons to swear—to get someone's attention and because it's fun. And those are probably the same two reasons why most people, certainly why *I*, quote and reference pop culture. Because it's fun and to get someone's attention. With the latter, the hope is that the reader has a similar sphere of experience, and that the mention will trigger in them the same pleasure node that made it fun for you. The trick is, if you do too much of anything purely because it's "fun," it can start to seem masturbatory. Too many digressions, too many relations of writing to baseball, to standup comedy, to hip-hop, and the class becomes all motherfucker—lazy, repetitive, obscene.

The other trick is, now that you've got someone's attention, what are you going to do with it?

USA Today described *Stand By Me* as, "A boy and his buddies set out on a hike to find a dead body." Which is of course exactly what the movie is about, and also not at all. I've taken to thinking of "set[ting] out on a hike to find a dead body" as the logic and theory; the deer scene, Vern's pennies, the pie-eating contest, etc., as the motherfuckers. One without the other doesn't work. On one hand, there's a driving force for the kids to go on a hike together, but nothing for us to fall in love with; on the other, a bunch of funny, relatable, memorable set pieces, but assorted scenes don't make a story.

On "Walking the Tracks," a bonus DVD extra, Stephen King relays,

> For a long time I thought, "I would love to be able to find a string to put on a lot of the childhood experiences that I remember, a lot of them are funny, and some of them are kinda sad" . . . and nothing came and nothing came, and what you do when nothing comes is you don't push you just put it aside and there came a day when I thought to myself, "If these guys go somewhere, if there's a *reason* for them to go somewhere, and do something, what could it be?" And I came up with the idea of them going down the train tracks, to look for the body of a kid, and I made up a situation whereby they would know the body was there and they could go and find it, and everything else follows from that.

26

When I told my wife my "I was twelve going on thirteen"/"I was x going on x+1" transition theory, her response was, "I think it's because kids always want to be older. They're always rounding up. They're *almost* thirteen, not just twelve."

Maybe my wife offered her own alternate idea because she thought my "going on" theory was overthought, academic bullshit. Or maybe she countered my theory with one of her own because that's what married couples do—they counter even when in essence they agree.

Or maybe it wasn't my attempted deconstruction of one of King's sentences that she was responding to, so much as my use of the word "transition." I'd been saying it a lot with regard to where we were in our relationship. Like, maybe we were transitioning out of marriage and into divorce. She seemed to take issue with this, while not necessarily disagreeing. Sometimes, I think about the inclusion of the prefix "ex" when referring to my wife. I find myself thinking about, whenever we talk about any kind of "remember when" stories, the end of Junot Díaz's "The Sun, The Moon, The Stars": "And that's when I know it's over. As soon as you start thinking about the beginning, it's the end."

At other times, I think ahead to us having worked through our problems, a future where we're not only still married, but in a much better, healthier marriage. In those moments, the thought of all this being put down in words, published, someone reading them, makes me very uncomfortable. Some days, I can't write, unable to let go of that discomfort; other days, I remember that first sentence of the very book I am writing about, King by way of Lachance imploring me—"The most important things are the hardest things to say"—and I don't let go of the discomfort so much as embrace it, telling myself maybe this is the best thing I've written.

Most likely, it's all somewhere in between.

Hopefully this book will be good, but doubtful one of the "most important things."

Probably my wife and I will work through it, and I'll be embarrassed about some of the personalness of this, but it won't be *that* embarrassing. And it will still have been a transitional phase. We weren't dealing with some of our problems, and then we did, and it was hard, but who hasn't struggled through a marriage. Marriage is hard.

Kids say they are almost thirteen, or twelve and three quarters, or *twelve going on thirteen*, because that's what kids do. They want to be older, they want to project themselves forward. The boys in "The Body" sometimes seem younger than twelve because, well, twelve is still pretty young. At other times, they seem older because twelve isn't actually as young as we sometimes remember it to be. And also because they want to be older. They swear and smoke, talk about both girls and their parents with a maturity that seems surprising, because they want to give off a sense of maturity. That's what you do when you're twelve. You seem both younger and older, because you are both. Because childhood itself is a transitional phase. You wish that you weren't just *going on* thirteen, but were already thirteen, fifteen. Maybe you don't yet want to be a grown up, but you certainly want to be grown up. And then you hit puberty. And then you have sex for the first time. And then you move out on your own. And then you see your first dead human being.

From Rebecca Lee's fantastic short story "Slatland:" "For every situation there is a proper distance. Growing up is just a matter of gaining perspective."

27

First date. First kiss. First job, first paycheck. First time you had sex. First real breakup. First road trip.

Firsts signify specific moments of before and after, while also demarcating an irreversible change in who we are. You can't return to the first half of the trailer, pre-"until now. . . ." Drew Barrymore in *Never Been Kissed*. ("She's never been hip. Never been cool. And she's never been sexy.") You can return to not being hip, or cool, or sexy, but not to *never been*. Becoming cool and then losing it isn't the same as never having been cool. You can't re-become a virgin. Every future road trip is colored with some of the memories of the first one.

First time you moved away from home. First time you lived on your own. First time you lived with a significant other. First date with the person who would become your spouse. First time you lived in a house of your own instead of apartment/dorm/your parent's house. First of your friends' weddings. First funeral. First time to another country.

Most of these just happen, often before you even realize it's your first time. You went to another country because someone planned the trip, or to visit a friend, or maybe because it seemed like a fun place to travel to. Probably not because you wanted specifically to lose your international-travel virginity. Or maybe you traveled a lot as a kid and never thought about it; maybe you just lived near Canada and crossed the border when in college so you could drink legally.

First tattoo.

If you're a writer, first publication. First book.

First time you saw your favorite movie.

First time you saw whatever it was that left an imprint on you deep enough that you remember it as having been the first time you saw that thing.

Some events are so important in your life, they can always be recalled with a clarity and ease that make them seem like not that long ago. And sometimes, an event need not be that important, sometimes there doesn't even need to be an event at all. That's just how time works. It flies when you're having fun. It speeds up as you get older. It folds in on itself; it's a flat circle. The past can often seem like both "a long time ago" and not that long at all.

First time you saw your favorite animal.

First time you read whatever would become your favorite book, the book you would end up returning to and rereading, the book you would most often recommend to people.

First time you tried to analyze something you loved.

First time you tried to write something so personal.

28

After seeing the deer, Gordie rejoins his friends, and they continue on their journey. In a summer that we'd already been told was the "driest and hottest since 1907," this morning in particular, Gordie remembers, may have been the hottest of all. So, when they see a pool of water just off the tracks they're following, they get excited. In *Stand By Me*, it's less culvert and more swamp, and they run into it trying to take a *shortest distance between two points is a straight line* shortcut through the woods, instead of following the tracks way out of their way. Swimming hole on hot day or swamp as shortcut isn't really important—what matters is, once they're in the water, they find it infested with leeches.

After removing the leeches from all over their bodies, the boys get dressed. Gordie then jumps ahead to a memory. "Fourteen years later I sold my first novel and made my first trip to New York." During that trip, Gordie tells his editor, Keith, that he wants to do "all the standard out-of-towner things." Radio City Music Hall, Times Square, the Empire State Building.[43]

---

43. "Fuck the World Trade Center, the building King Kong climbed in 1933 is always gonna be the tallest one in the world for me," Lachance parenthetically asides, now an odd reminder of pre-9/11 times.

The two of them take the Staten Island Ferry and, looking over the rail down into the water, Gordie sees "scores of used condoms floating on the mild swells." While Keith reads Gordie's pained reaction as disgust, the condoms actually remind Gordie of the leeches. "For one second I was literally *in* the past, pausing halfway up that embankment and looking back at the burst leech." Gordie tells us what he'd wanted to tell Keith, in perhaps the most "on writing" sentence in the story: "*The only reason anyone writes stories is so they can understand the past and get ready for some future mortality.*" What he says to Keith instead is "I was thinking of something else, that's all." And then the chapter ends the same as the novella began: *The most important things are the hardest things to say.*

I've spent the last year or so being more introspective than I probably ever have been in my life. Thinking about why "The Body" and *Stand By Me* have had such an effect on me has led to me thinking about my own life; about the way I teach, both as a process toward improving, and as a necessary evil for job applications; and about my marriage, ferreting out and putting language to our struggles, so as to know what to work on, and how.

In the first chapter of this book, I wrote, "At least a small part of me fears what might happen when applying analysis to something held so close to the heart, by asking either too many questions, or maybe just the *right* questions." I didn't really know what that meant, but it sounded good, literary.

It also let me off the hook for laziness in inquiry. Then, while doing research for this book, I uncovered that, when he was young, a kid Stephen King had been playing with had been run over by a freight train. And, later, there was another incident, a boating accident where someone had died. King's childhood friend, Chris Chesley, recounted:

> A friend of mine said to me and Steve, "Do you want to see a dead body?" "Why not?" we said. "It'd be great! No problem there!" When we got to Runaround Pond, they had dragged the body up, with lights shining on it. They had not covered up the corpse yet.
>
> It was an educational experience for all of us. It wasn't a pleasant sight.[44]

My initial response when I discovered all this was annoyance. I didn't want to know what had or hadn't *actually happened*. I liked that the novella *felt* real, like something that had actually happened, but I also wanted to hold on to the idea that maybe none of it did, that maybe it was all King's imagination. It can be fun to take apart a magic trick and figure out how it actually works, but it also ruins the magic of the trick.

But then, the discovery of this information sank in, and it turned out it didn't really matter—it didn't affect *something held so close to the heart*. If anything, that initial annoyance turned into appreciation for how King took something from life, but crafted it into something else.

I've spent a lot of my marriage, a lot of my *life*, not asking questions, at least not aloud, not saying *the most important things*, because they are *the hardest things to say*. Because of the initial annoyance. Because of the discomfort or fight it may lead to. Because you can trick yourself into thinking that not saying something means it doesn't exist.

29

On first viewing, you don't yet know the full affect of what you're watching, but with each subsequent viewing, the beginning of *Stand By Me* is incredibly sad.

The movie is told in bookends, a technique that, together with voiceovers, utilizes two of the most clichéd narrative methods in moviemaking. They almost always feel manipulative, cheesy, and often are entirely unnecessary in telling a story. However, it's the "almost" before the "always" that allows their continued existence, the exception that proves the rule.

Stand By Me opens with Richard Dreyfuss as adult Gordie sitting alone in his Land Rover. The camera zooms in, and he looks sad, pensive, and then there is a cut to a newspaper lying on the passenger seat. *The Oregonian*, Wednesday, September 4, 1985, the headline reading, "Attorney Christopher Chambers Fatally Stabbed In Restaurant." If you have already seen the movie, you know that Chris Chambers is River Phoenix's character. The headline tells you that he became an attorney—proving Gordie's pep talk to Chris at one point in their adventure that you can overcome the odds and do anything you put your mind to.

But it also reminds us that not all stories have happy endings. Furthering the heartbreak is the echo of Phoenix's own early death, an overdose at age twenty-three.

I just finished watching the movie again, and the beginning still leaves me choked up. It reminds me that joy comes with sadness, and this mixture of the two emotional extremes is one of the reasons why I come back to *Stand By Me* over and over again. A part of me looks forward to that camera panning to the newspaper on the seat, to the welling of grief I know the movie is going to produce in me.

We do this with pop culture all the time. "What came first," the protagonist of Nick Hornby's *High Fidelity* asks (similarly, in both book and movie). "The music or the misery. Did I listen to music because I was miserable? Or was I miserable because I listened to music?"

One of Marc Maron's frequent talking points on his wonderful podcast, *WTF*, is a paraphrasing of something Harry Shearer once told him. "The reason comedians do what they do is to try to control why people laugh at them." Stand-up comedians are rarely the cool kids in high school, and it's not a stretch to imagine that most of them grew up as outcasts, being picked on and laughed at. Their power comes not in avoiding being laughed at, but in controlling when it will happen.

I'd say the same rule applies to sadness. We often admit the power of crying after it's happened and we're out the other side, but we seem to spend so much time holding it in. Or, I guess I should say, *I* spend so much time holding it in. Generally, if I feel tears coming on, I try to hold them back because, as Maron said in referring to comedians, "I think we're all afraid of being embarrassed or being ashamed or being rejected."

But I also hold it in because tears are often precipitated by something incredibly sad—death, breakups—and if I feel that, if I hold back the tears, I can hold back the sadness, too, I can will the bad news to not happen, even un-happen . . . or at least I can pretend.

But what if there were a way to direct these feelings? To not deny the power of the emotion, but embrace it. Not to avoid it, but to control it.

Watch Nirvana's MTV *Unplugged*. Or Tracy Chapman perform "Stand By Me" on one of the last episodes of *The Late Show with David Letterman*. Or, speaking of the final weeks of Letterman, watch Norm Macdonald tell him, "I know that Mr. Letterman is not for the mawkish and he has no truck for the sentimental, BUT, if something is true, it isn't sentimental. And I say in truth, I love you."

Listen to Elliott Smith and bathe in that feeling. Or double down and watch Luke Wilson's suicide scene in *The Royal Tenenbaums* while Smith's "Needle in the Hay" plays on the soundtrack.

But then listen to something else and pull yourself out of it.

Or queue up *Stand By Me*, and embrace the sadness of the world as Richard Dreyfuss reads about Chris Chambers' fatal stabbing. Appreciate the chills running through your body, the goose bumps prickling down your arms.

Robert J. Wiersema, in *Walk Like a Man: Coming of Age with the Music of Bruce Springsteen*, writes, "Nostalgia is, by its very nature, bittersweet, the happiest memories laced with melancholy. It's that combination, that opposition of forces, that makes it so compelling. People, places, events, times: we miss them, and there's a pleasure in the missing and a sadness in the love."

30

In suburban Ann Arbor, there is a large commercial real estate complex known as Domino's Farms Office Park. The world headquarters of Domino's Pizza, the park is, according to its website, "one of the nation's most architecturally significant and recognizable office structures." Inspired by the design principles of Frank Lloyd Wright, the complex has been described (the website also tells us) by Yale art historian Vincent Scully as "the ultimate example of [Wright's] Prairie Style house type." The campus includes 270 acres of mostly open land, encompassing manicured lawns and garden beds, cultivated fields, grazing pastures, and natural-habitat water courses. There is also a petting zoo that my wife and I used to take her daughter to when she was younger.

For me, however, Domino's Farms is best known for its signature herd of American bison. During our years living here in Ann Arbor, my wife and I have often driven to Domino's Farms just to watch the buffalo. It's a calming experience. My wife always feels more relaxed when around animals, and, of course, buffalo are our animal. As Gordie writes about seeing the deer, "it seems a lesser thing written down, damn near inconsequential. But for me it was the best part of that trip,

the cleanest part, and it was a moment I found myself return-ing to, almost helplessly, when there was trouble in my life."
I too have found myself returning to the buffalo at Domino's Park, *almost helplessly, when there was trouble in my life.*

Before attending *Stand By Me* Day, I took a trip down to Indianapolis to see a reading. A quicker, shorter excuse to hang out with friends, to get out of town for a night. We saw the reading, we went out drinking, and I drove home the next morning. Returning to Ann Arbor, I drove straight to Domino's Farms. I don't know if to avoid the apartment I was subletting for a few months, like my freshman-self killing hours in the computer lab to avoid going home, or if I purely wanted to see the buffalo. It was sunny out and I wanted to take advantage of it; I knew, once home, I would likely stay there for the night, and in my apartment building, I couldn't enjoy the sun by sitting on our deck and reading, or even doing yard work. So I went to see the buffalo.

In addition to the buffalo, Domino's Farms is also home to numerous native waterfowl and other exotic farm animals. There are cattle, a Texas longhorn. There are a couple animals that I sometimes liked to feed that look like donkeys. I had never known for sure what they were, but this time, I saw a sign, or maybe I'd just never noticed it before:

BAUDET DE POITOU – (POITOU)

The Poitou was developed side by side with the Mulassier (draft horse) for the sole purpose of pro-ducing draft mules (donkey crossed with horse) of exceptional quality. After World War II, the need for draft animals was greatly reduced and their numbers fell drastically, almost to extinction. By 1977 only 44 donkeys of any age could be counted. Today, through careful breeding, there are as many as 400 purebred Poitou Donkeys.

I parked my car on the side of the road, grabbed a book and got out. I walked toward the Poitou, pulling some of the tall grass and weeds from outside their fenced-in area. They came over to the fence and took the weeds from my out-stretched arm; they got close and let me pet them.

Across the road that drives through the Domino Farms complex is another fence that opens out into the 100 acres where the herd of buffalo roam. The buffalo were nearer the fence than I'd ever seen them. I crossed the street and slowly headed toward them, careful to not frighten them away. As I approached, they started walking away, so I stopped. They stopped as well, started eating grass where they were, and then continued to wander. I slowly followed the walkway next to the fence, and this time the buffalo stayed where they were, watching me but continuing to graze. Finally, I'd walked into an open patch of grass, where I sat down and watched the buf-falo as they watched me. There were baby bison, who I watched suckle milk from there mothers, and when not feeding, they looked almost like they wanted to run over and play with me; there were adolescent bison who looked to be more curious about my existence, but less like they wanted to have anything to do with me; and there were the adults, mostly disinterested in me, watching only that I didn't come near their children, nor their children toward me. For the next few hours, I sat there, alternately reading my book and watching the buffalo.

31

Shortly after moving to California, I went to see the Mark Wahlberg movie, *Rock Star*, with the girl I'd moved with from Seattle. It's not a very good film, but it's entertaining enough, in that way that most not-very-good Mark Wahlberg movies are. At the end, Chris Cole, the character played by Wahlberg, gives up his rock star life and moves to Seattle to become a post-grunge singer/songwriter. I remember feeling almost embarrassed by how emotionally I reacted to the ending. It's cheesy and cliché, but maybe cheesy and cliché doesn't have to be pejorative. Or, maybe they do, but that doesn't mean they can't be embraced, can't affect you. Chris had found peace, and happiness in Seattle, the city I'd just moved away from, the *first time* I'd really moved away from home. There's something about seeing a movie filmed in your hometown and recognizing locations. That's the Fremont troll. That's Gasworks Park. That's where RKCNDY was, where I went to so many hardcore shows in high school and college.

I wouldn't say I was homesick, but I wouldn't say I wasn't, either. I was enjoying living in California; still, at the time, enjoying living with my girlfriend. I didn't want to move back to Seattle, but seeing it there up on the screen, seeing Marky Mark end up happy in the city that I associated with being happy in, felt . . . *good*.

Maybe what I'm talking about here, at its core, is the same idea that I'm getting at when trying to dig into nostalgia. It's the same as, or at least similar to, some of the pleasures of meta-fiction, which themselves are the same as a recognizable artistic universe, be it Tarantino's or *Star Wars or* Kevin Smith's. It's an artist's work existing in a unified universe, and it's the Easter eggs that can be found within that universe. It's the pleasure of recognition, the enjoyment of an inside joke. The joy of a great friendship, a group of friends. The comfort of the familiar. It's "The Body" being set in Castle Rock; it's Stephen King's Gordon Lachance having published the same number of books as King himself, books that also happen to be about "people who can do such things as read minds and precognit the future."

32

After spending a day and a night in Brownsville by myself, my friends arrived in town, driving down from Tacoma together. We went out to eat,[45] caught up. We went to the store for groceries and beer. And, of course, we watched *Stand By Me*.

The following day, we went on the same walking tour of the town I had gone on alone my first night. We excitedly pointed at things we recognized from the movie, we quoted lines to one another, we took photos reenacting scenes. We were like tourists embracing the most pleasurable aspects of tourism.

Brownsville is a small town, and after we completed our walking tour, there wasn't a lot to do. So, back to my phone, with the idea of finding a swimming hole. Which we did, and which is where we spent the rest of the day—exploring the river, swimming, jumping off rocks and felled trees into deep pools we could barely touch the bottom of. It felt like a scene out of a movie, perhaps a forced simile because we were in the

---

45. At the Mexican Restaurant, downtown's only restaurant other than the Brownsville Saloon.

town for the annual day celebrating a movie filmed there, but how else to describe four friends spending hours enjoying a swimming hole with complete childlike abandon?

The next day was *Stand By Me* Day. We awoke and went to Irby's Billiards (nee the Brownsville Saloon) for a blueberry pancake breakfast. Afterward, we went on a guided walking tour through town, though we learned little more than we had from our self-guided tour the day before. We each got *Cobras* "razor-blade tattooed" (face-paint style) on our arms. Later in the afternoon, there was to be a presentation by Katherine Wilson, the local casting director for *Stand By Me*, and this was, I presumed, where I would get the most information about Brownsville as a shooting location for the movie. Only, by this point, I realized I wasn't really there for research. "The Body" isn't really about finding Ray Brower's body, but about the four boys; *Stand By Me* Day, for me, wasn't really about this book I was writing, but instead was an excuse to fly across the country and hang out with old friends. So, we returned to the swimming hole.

Wes and Mark had to drive back to Tacoma that evening, but Brooks had a train ticket to return the next afternoon. So the two of us returned to the Brownsville Saloon (now no longer Irby's Ballroom) for a drink and a burger. One drink turned into a second. We started talking to the bartender; we met a local blueberry farmer, such an oddly obvious connection to *Stand By Me* that it didn't even occur to me until later. We queued up songs on the jukebox and the bartender seemed impressed by Brooks's taste in music. He insisted on buying us another round. Eventually the blueberry farmer left, as did the waitress drinking there on her day off. The other patrons left, the cook left. The bartender gave Brooks money to feed the jukebox. Brooks played Sylvan Esso, who I'd never heard of before. We shared a round of shots with the bartender. He told us how hard it was to be a gay man in such a small, rural town. I thought about how "the most important things are the hardest things to say." I said something about how hard marriage can be. He said he'd lived in Portland, an obviously much more LGBTQ-friendly city, but that he preferred Brownsville because he preferred the slower pace, the community of people. I drunkenly echoed the power of community. I said I was there in town for *Stand By Me* Day; I was there in town with my friends.

I had gone to *Stand By Me* Day for a host of reasons— to see friends, to travel, to do research for this book—but, if I'm being totally honest, I went in large part just so that I could say I'd gone. I could take and post pictures on social media of several iconic locations: the bridge that is featured in the movie; the split in the road where, at the end of the film, Teddy veers off from the group in one direction, Vern in the other; the tree that no longer holds a treehouse, but is recognizable nonetheless. At the same time, the trip was the highlight of my summer, because I had been there with three great friends.

If, before, I quoted "All happy families are alike," I can quote here, too, "It was the best of times, it was the worst of times." It has, in many ways, been one of my worst years of my life, but in other ways, it has been one of the best. I've spent a lot of time with friends, sharing with them my marriage struggles, which has only made these friendships stronger. I've analyzed "The Body" in ways that the part of me that never really loved being a student often avoids, which has led to this book, helped me become a better teacher, and unlocked some of the issues I've been having with the novel I am trying to finish. I've worked on my marriage in ways that I had been avoiding, ways that nearly always felt easier at the time but ultimately led to the hole my wife and I had dug for ourselves.

The four boys in "The Body" go on a search for a dead body so that they can let the authorities know where it is, and then they'll be celebrated, they'll be *famous*. In the end, though, they leave the body where they found it, burying it under leaves, and then a week later, someone makes an anonymous call. They don't get the credit. It doesn't matter. What matters was the trip itself—two days away from town, away from their parents, telling each other stories, having a run-in with the dog at the scrapyard, the horrible-at-the-moment-but-a-great-story-later leeches attack. Two days of just being friends.

33

After the deer, and the leeches (and Gordie thinking about the leeches and fainting), we get another chapter of reflection from adult Gordie. He surprises us with the revelation that he is the only one of the four boys who is still alive. He doesn't tell us how or when each one died, only that "they didn't die in the woods or on the railroad tracks; nobody dies in this story."

Continuing to reflect, Gordie again emphasizes the importance of those two days in the woods. He tells us, and also seems to be discovering for himself, mid-reflection, "This was something on par with getting laid for the first time, or going into the Army, or buying your first bottle of liquor." Again with the firsts, the before and the after. "There's a high ritual to all fundamental events," Gordie continues, "the rites of passage, the magic corridor where the change happens." Gordie is speaking of the moments in our lives that we may not think much of at the time, but which turn out to have great meaning. The moments that change us, that make us who we are. These fundamental events, these rites of passage, these magic corridors, are important not in and of themselves, but for the change that happens within them, and by extension, within us.

And then we're back in1960, and Gordie and Chris and Vern and Teddy find the body. "Chris looked into my eyes," Gordie remembers, "his face set and stern—an adult's face." If "The Body" is about the transition of twelve *going on* thirteen, if it is a coming of age story, it's literally in that moment described on Chris's face. And then Ace Merrill and his gang show up: "Well what the fuck do you know about this?"

Ace (and Eyeball, and Charlie Hogan, and Vern's brother Billy) are barely present throughout most of "The Body." The story is written from Gordie's point of view, and he doesn't know what the members of Ace's gang are up to, that they are searching for a body as well. The gang members have larger roles in *Stand By Me*, mainly because movies need antagonists, the story is told less explicitly from Gordie's POV, despite Richard Dreyfuss's narration, and because if you have 1986 Kiefer Sutherland in your movie, you take as much advantage of that as possible. But in the novella, Ace and his gang show up after a long absence, and Gordie drops the classic, "Suck my fat one, you cheap dime store hood" line on Ace, and Chris fires "the pistol he had hawked out of his old man's dresser," scaring off the gang.[46]

In the final chapters, we learn that Ace and Fuzzy later jump Gordie on the street, beating him up, breaking his nose and fingers. Chris gets his arm broken in two places by his brother, Eyeball, who also leaves Chris's face "looking like a Canadian sunrise." Vern and Teddy "took their lumps, too."

The retaliation feels like one more aspect of giving "The

---

46. In *Stand By Me*, it is Gordie who fires the pistol, giving him a little more agency, keeping him a little more front and center as protagonist.

Body" resonance, adding a sense of realism to the boys' defiance of Ace and company. Life is rarely easy, endings are rarely "happily ever after." But, at the moment of the boy's discovery of the body, and then the gang's arrival from nowhere, Ace et al prove to the boys that it wasn't really about Ray Brower at all. Gordie doesn't want Ace to "get" Brower, but he doesn't want his friends and himself to get him either. The plan had been to find the body and to get a reward or famous, to be heroes. In the end, they leave the body there, return to town.

34

"Me?" the final chapter of "The Body" asks. "I'm a writer now, like I said," Gordon Lachance answers. Stephen King answers. I answer as well. A writer and a teacher.

Early this semester, I cancelled a few classes to go on a short reading tour with two friends. The tour started at the Pygmalion Festival, in Champaign, Illinois, a music festival that has grown to include readings, a lit crawl and a book fair. I have gone every year since I graduated from grad school in Champaign and moved back to Ann Arbor. It's an excuse to sell some books, to see some readings and music, and to catch up with friends that still live in the town where I lived for three years.

I invited Brooks to go along. The two of us had had so much fun in Brownsville, and I thought he would enjoy both the music and literary halves of the festival. His enthusiasm, support, and encouragement of my literary life (he has read most, if not everything, I have written, and has represented *Hobart* at multiple book fairs in Seattle, proving to be one of the most enthusiastic and effective sellers and promoters of our journals and books) is matched only by his enthusiasm for music.

One of the highlights of the festival was seeing Sylvan Esso with Brooks, who had turned me on to their album while we were in Brownsville a few months earlier. After the concert, a friend said she'd seen me in the crowd, next to a "super fan." "I know!" I said. "That's my friend! He came out from Seattle just for the festival!!"

Over the next three days, Brooks and I ate some great food, and saw some amazing authors. We spent most of one day at a book fair held in my favorite bar from grad school, and then went to a reading in another bar where I read pieces of this very book to a packed house, including one of my favorite living writers. And to top it all off, we saw Run the Jewels, perhaps my favorite group of the last year, a performance that led to one of the most surreal moments of my life: a few songs into the group's set, a guy next to me tapped on my shoulder and yelled over the crowd noise, "I loved your *Stand By Me* reading!"

But, even among all those moments, the one that most stands out was something Run the Jewels' El-P said in between songs. He thanked us all for being there, said how great of a crowd we were. How they'd have to come back to Champaign. How much fun they were having, how great the tour they were currently in the middle of had been going. Then he said something about how great it was to be there on the stage with his best friend, Killer Mike, the other half of RTJ. And it gave me chills. In a way I certainly didn't expect in the middle of a rap concert, and in a way that it has a number of times since when thinking about or retelling the moment to friends. It is standard fare to tell an audience that they're great, that you, the band, love the town you're in. And maybe it's likewise cliché to say how great it is to share the stage with your friends, but one of the reasons the Run the Jewels albums are my favorites of the past few years, one of the reasons why they are among my favorite live performances I've seen, is because it is obvious they are having fun. That they love the music they're making, they're enjoying the success they're finally having, both rappers later in their careers. But maybe most of all they're each sharing that enjoyment and success with their best friend.

I started this book writing about nostalgia, because it is one of my personal go-to's—in conversation, and in my writing—and because it seemed like a good argument to make about why "The Body," and by extension, *Stand By Me*, work. And yet my very first memory of ever watching the movie, the first thing I wrote about for this very book, is my dad telling me that the movie might be a little mature for me but that it was worth it because it's about friendship.

I think the reason I gravitate toward nostalgia is that I've had such great friends in my life. I like thinking and joking about the nineties in large part because I like remembering hanging out with my high school friends; living in Champaign and getting an MFA hold a place in my heart not having anything to do with writing, but because of the friends I made while there.

It may sound cheesy to sum it up so simplistically, to render it so emotionally bare, but as Gordie Lachance, as Stephen King, remind us, the most important things are the hardest things to say. And so, yes, unlike Gordie Lachance, I *did* have friends later on like the ones I had when I was twelve. But the age of the question isn't the important part of the sentiment. Ultimately, my takeaway is something more alone the lines of: I'm not sure what in life is better than one's friends.

Jesus, is anything?

The *Bookmarked* Series

John Knowles' *A Separate Peace* by Kirby Gann

Kurt Vonnegut's *Slaughterhouse-Five* by Curtis Smith

Christina Stead's *The Man Who Loved Children* by Paula Bomer

Malcolm Lowry's *Under the Volcano* by David W. Ryan

F. Scott Fitzgerald's *The Great Gatsby* by Jaime Clarke

Mark Danielewski's *House of Leaves* by Michael Seidlinger

Larry McMurtry's *The Last Picture Show* by Steve Yarbrough